Men and Dogs

Martin Hamer

First published in UK 2012 by Hamer 20th Century Books (Publishing).

Copyright © 2012 Martin Hamer

All rights reserved. No part of this publication may be reproduced, stored in a retrieval system, or transmitted, in any form or by any means, electronic or mechanical, photocopying, recording or otherwise, without the prior permission of both the copyright owner and the above publisher.

ISBN 978-0-9537875-4-8

Distributed by Hamer 20th Century Books, Springfield, Woodsetts S81 8QD.

Email mj.hamer@btinternet.com

Acknowledgements
Rex Carter *Men and Gods*
Whitwell Local History Group

Printed and bound in Worksop UK by Bayliss Printing Company Limited.

Men and Dogs

1.

Delgatty believed, in his dream that night, he was at Brownhills Greyhound Stadium and it was black. Gradually lights arose dimly from the restaurant frontage and the lamps around the track. The circuit itself was as big as a reservoir. Not another soul was present; not even the soul of a dog.

All at once there was a the sound of a single bugle and the lights blossomed with exaggerated force. Delgatty was temporarily blinded but then could just make out a procession of men, women and a couple of horses in front of him; horses fortified with something like chain mail. The steam of horse shit permeated the hot air.

A crowd began to clap and then to roar a welcome to him. A band added its chaotic music to the heat. He automatically removed his hat in acknowledgement. He inclined his head towards the cap in his hand. It was a black montera; a matador's hat. He put it back on his head. In his other hand he held a large yellow and purple capote; a bullfighter's cape.

He saw himself, as a spectator might from the heights of the arena, in a suit of lights; sky blue jacket and pantalons with intricate, gold embroidery. Beside him were two other matadors, both women.

A woman, a beautiful woman he did not know, held her black hat in her hand and saluted the crowd. Harriet was the other matador and she flared her nostrils as she inhaled the blaring music and nodded regally to the shouts of the crowd. Both women looked spectacular; Harriet in a dazzling suit and the other woman in white blouse, short, blue suede skirt and platform shoes.

Each matador was accompanied by three banderilleros whose job it is to thrust their decorated darts into the bull's shoulders. Delgatty forced a steely smile at each of his own team or cuadrilla in turn; Tony, Mary and a black man he did not know. They all looked beautiful in their silver outfits but the black guy stood godlike in the ring gorging on this admiration from the throng. The two females, Delgatty saw briefly, were supported, amongst others he did not recognise, by Skinner, scratching his arms as usual, and a young Japanese woman.

The procession evaporated in the dream and the vision now zoomed in on the picadores. Judge and Dexter hove into view, relaxed and smiling on their respective armoured horses; their vertical lances borne symmetrically.

The strong light turned to blistering, bright sunshine and Delgatty found himself craving the shade. The crowd, which by now must have been twenty thousand or more, were on their feet applauding him, crying out their praises and throwing flowers into the ring. He doffed the montera again and bowed theatrically to the arena, turning himself so he faced, at intervals, the whole of the circular stadium.

Esther Marie stood silently behind him, bearing a sword.

Each of the toreros strode confidently to the front of the once Royal Box and bowed, not to Franco who had been present on Delgatty's visit to an actual bullfight, but bowed instead to someone who looked like a Roman emperor in his toga and laurel wreath. Delgatty recognised him as Cyril Laverman, the principal bookmaker at Perry Barr dog track. One of Laverman's heavies, in black sunglasses, sat next to him.

Father Ryan and an Asian man stood behind Laverman's box, their hands clasped as if in prayer. The easily-recognisable Punch stood next to the holy men and was speaking into the ear of the near-blind Cadman, describing the scene to him.

The band stopped playing. An occasional shout came from the arena as most of the people settled into their stone, bench seats and became virtually silent. Delgatty and his cuadrilla were the first to fight and had the bullring to themselves. The picadores and the others had disappeared.

The doors were flung open in the sunny side of the ring and the bull, all fifteen hundred pounds of black muscle, charged into the arena seemingly a yard off the ground and at thirty miles an hour.

It was more mammoth than bull.

Jesus Christ. This fucking thing will kill us all.

Tony leapt behind the callejón which in English we call an alley. The bull slammed into the wooden structure and Delgatty, on the edge of the shade, caught the stink of its wild breath and he wanted to choke.

Mary and the black man moved in close to the bull and distracted him away from the alley with their magenta and gold capes, getting close to him, confusing him. Tony emerged from his refuge and joined them in an episode of passes which engendered applause and whistles of approval.

Then it was Delgatty's turn to engage with this beast. He too made a number of passes. One particularly artistic pass, a veronica, won the cheers of the whole stadium and Delgatty, although fear ran through him like an icy brook, felt as though he was Nijinsky himself, dancing at the Bolshoi.

The bugle signalled the re-entry of the picadores. Judge stationed himself and his armoured horse in the sunny part of the arena. Dexter and his armoured nag crossed the sand to the shade whilst Tony, Mary and the black banderillero continued to divert the bull so it did not get a long run at the horse. As Dexter had taken up his position the bull saw him and began to charge at his animal at such a pace that the horse, had he struck it, would probably have sailed into the crowd. But the three banderilleros did their job well. Mary and Tony danced their slight frames in and out of the passage of the animal, curbing its speed by strategic and artistic use of their capes.

The bull was now alongside the horse and began to lift it off the ground with his enormous head and horns. Dexter sat tight and shoved his lance into its neck muscle, drawing blood for the first time. The bull continued to attack the horse and turned it on its side, casting Dexter to the ground. The banderilleros quickly intervened, allowing the horse to get to its feet and Dexter to scramble his bulk into the callejón.

The nag transmogrified into a mighty grey, almost white, racehorse and sped across the ring, making his exit by leaping the doors to the bull corridor like Pegasus himself.

Delgatty, in the real world, had only attended one bullfight, although one bullfight is actually six bullfights with three different matadors each fighting two bulls. He had only been fully impressed by one. Two of the six had been a mess. Either the bull wouldn't fight, in which case the president of the festival had declared the fight void and a small herd of cattle had entered the arena to escort the bull to the ignominy of the slaughter house, or the matador had just screwed up in one way or another. The other three were OK. It was like football; many games are just OK or scrappy and leave the crowd disappointed. Then there's the few you remember all your life.

This was a proper fight with a bold and dangerous bull and the whole arena knew it. The banderilleros had done their job and the bull now carried their barbed sticks in his bleeding shoulders.

Delgatty entered the ring alone and faced his opponent with a small red cape or muleta and a light, wooden sword for the final movements of this bloody ballet. The actual sword remained with sword-page, Esther Marie.

He stared at the swinging dewlaps, blunt muzzle and huge horns of the bull. The creature pawed the ground and plunged forward. Delgatty made one pass, two, three passes and the crowd was ecstatic.

The animal stood in the dead centre of the ring and Delgatty went towards him with cape and fake sword behind his back. He bowed to the applauding assembly. He looked into the eyes of the deadly creature.

Hey! Torro!

The bull stared back at him. They had an intuitive knowledge of each other across the species. Delgatty knew the bull was aware of its mortality but the animal could not believe it would be here and now. Not in this sun. Not in his prime. This was how a young man would feel who had wandered, on a summer evening, into a group of thugs bearing knives and intent on killing him for no reason.

In this stillness a pair of vultures winged in from the blue and settled on the turrets of what had now transformed into a Medieval arena. There was total silence.

Delgatty walked across the ring to Esther Marie. He held out his hand for the sword. She shook her head. He asked her a question.

Clemency?

Of course. Always.

With the bull still in the middle of the ring, Delgatty walked to the president's box and signalled to the foremost bookmaker at Perry Barr dogs that he wanted a pardon for the animal. Cyril Laverman stood, applauded and waved his agreement. The public left no doubt as to their concurrence.

The vultures took clumsy flight.

The bull was gradually ushered from the arena by the banderilleros. His wounds would be attended to. He left the ring, a hero for a life at stud. He also quit Delgatty's dream.

2.

There is a track going downhill and shaded by deathly yew trees. It leads to the bottom of Creswell Craggs where the spirits of Ice Age Man flit amongst the ghosts of hyenas and bears. The caves remain daubed with his paintings but the muses that inspired him fifteen thousand years ago are now turned to jackdaws and magpies.

Delgatty stirred a number of these same muses into flight as he emerged from the beaten track, the leads of a brace of greyhounds in each hand. The breath of the five of them merged into one vaporous cloud in the March, morning cold.

He sat down on a rock and the dogs watched as he took out a small cigar, lit it with a match and blew the first smoke of the day into the thin, blue air. The greyhounds stood, one dog resting his head on the bitch's back, the other two young dogs from Queenie's first litter stood independently, open-mouthed and breathing a little heavily after their exertions. They each admired this piece of work that was man.

He noticed the bitch was showing the early signs of being in season; a nuisance because she was only just recovering from a slight wrist injury and hadn't run for over a month. He would have to separate her from Rex when they got back to the kennels. Rex would of course pine for his mate but he'd only be in the next kennel, and only for a few weeks.

Anyway at least you'll be able to get on the bed. She won't let you will she? She makes you sleep on the floor, doesn't she?

Rex smiled at Delgatty and yawned with embarrassment at being singled out for comment. The tails of the dogs swung gently with pleasure. Rex at seven years was retired and was Esther Marie's pet. In his racing days he had been officially called Prancing Oedipus.

Queenie's racing name, registered with The National Greyhound Racing Club or NGRC, was Atalanta. She was only four years old and, although she had already whelped a litter to Derby winner Lucifer Star, still had another few months racing in her before she would be retired finally as a brood bitch. Despite being a hypochondriac, the bitch could be relied on to win three or four races every few months and Delgatty's bets on her more or less paid for the upkeep of his small set-up.

From time to time she would drop her shoulder as she walked. Delgatty could never find a sore spot nor could Dalgleish, the Scottish vet Delgatty relied on; the only vet he would consult.

There's nothing wrong with her. I've given her a numbing injection and she's still walking lame. It's in her head.

When it wasn't in her head and she had walked and galloped soundly for a week or so, Delgatty would back her. Not for fortunes. He might have a hundred quid at 3/1 or something like that.

They returned to the house through the large bottle-green gates he had left open. The curved gates were a work of art in themselves. They were set in a semi-circular, stone wall which had Tuscan arch windows. Italy was making an architectural impression in Derbyshire. The Romans had been there a couple of thousand years ago so why not The Tuscans?

Delgatty's mother Phyllis and his father Luke had stayed for a few weeks in 1971 and Luke had asked if he could embellish the wall in this Italian way. He wasn't a woodworker by profession. He was a vicar but he couldn't wait to get home from the Parish Church Council and the Chapter meetings to his lathe and his Kensitas.

Phyllis and Luke would often accommodate a tramp or someone in distress in their large vicarage and the kids would, on occasions, come home from school to find some new arrival locked in the bathroom, their smelly underclothes and shirts piled by the washing machine in the kitchen for his mother to try and restore to something like freshness. The newly-clean stranger would appear, dressed in one of his mother's dresses or his father's old suits.

Only till they get on their feet.

By October 1972 both parents were dead; killed in a freak accident. Returning through a thunder storm from a harvest festival supper in their Austin A40, they were struck by a tree crashing from the heavens and cleaving the car and its occupants.

They worshipped Heaven and now they must themselves be worshipped.

Delgatty said the words automatically.

He took off Queenie's lead and collar and put her into her kennel. The six kennels within this large stone outhouse, built at right angles to the house, Delgatty and his father had made of breeze block to about four foot and then slatted up to the ceiling, giving the dogs plenty of air and vision. Occasionally you would have a dog who would chew this kennel frame and, rather than leave the animal in a muzzle, it was best to make the wood as inaccessible as possible. Father and son had made an excellent job between them.

The finest kennels in the land.

Delgatty put the two young, fawn dogs into their separate kennels. Bobby and Frankie were, as yet, officially un-named. Although the dogs were brothers and of a seemingly gentle disposition, the males of the species should never be kennelled together unless muzzled. He remembered seeing the damage that two dogs can cause each other. There were two full brothers at a major NGRC track who had been together all their lives but muzzled as they got older.

One Saturday after racing the kennel maid forgot to muzzle them and they were locked away for the night. Delgatty was there the next morning to walk a couple of his own dogs and he was shocked to see the torn hind quarters of one of the dogs and a piece of flesh a foot wide hanging loose from the other dog's shoulder to his rib cage. They must have given way to the muzzled, pent-up anger of their last year together. Delgatty was glad he didn't have to explain to the owner.

He tied Rex's lead to the slats and forked off the old straw from the platform bed. He swilled out the floor of the old dog's temporary abode with disinfectant and swept it clean with a yard brush. Delgatty broke a section of a bale of straw and spread it on Rex's wooden bed. Then he threw a couple of handfuls of fine sawdust on the floor to absorb the urine; probably not necessary in Rex's case as dogs are generally much more house proud than bitches and rarely piss near their sleeping quarters.

All done now Rex. Get on your bed.

Rex liked to jump. He leapt up and down on the spot. He'd always done it, hence his racing name, Prancing Oedipus.

Delgatty spoke more firmly but couldn't keep the smile out of his voice as he sang.

He jumped so high. He jumped so high then he'd lightly step down.

Get on your bed now, Mr. Bojangles.

And the dog obeyed as did the other three even though they weren't being addressed directly.

The kennels smelled musty from the old straw. He bundled it into a plastic bag to burn in the garden and crossed to the small timber garage at the end of the driveway. The door scraped on the stones as he dragged it open.

Bales of straw were stacked in the rafters of this old outhouse. He eased himself past the dusty old Vauxhall Estate to reach some kindling. He patted the bonnet.

Two more weeks and you'll be back on the road girl.

The previous March Delgatty had been in the dock.

And in view of the amount of alcohol in your blood and your absolute lack of co-operation with the police, I have no hesitation in disqualifying you from driving for twelve months and fining you one hundred pounds.

It had been two in the morning and he had decided to risk driving the mile home from Creswell. He wasn't even drunk. In fact he never really got drunk. Sure he drank, he drank a lot, but if he felt he was going to be sorry in the morning he would always stop. He had dogs to do and miles to walk.

The police thing was another matter. Lots of coppers from down south appeared during the strikes and it was just natural antipathy that made him *unco-operative.*

That and the fact that Delgatty was something of an anarchic bastard.

He burnt the straw and wet sawdust in a corner of the garden, the light smoke drifting over the wall and into the adjacent field.

He took a key from his trouser pocket and unlocked the door to the back of the house, washed his hands in the steel kitchen sink, tore off a piece of kitchen roll to dry them and chucked it in the unlit boiler to burn later. He walked into the large downstairs room which had been two rooms he and his dad had knocked into one. They'd boxed in the RSJ to create another beam.

Delgatty took a couple of mugs from the cupboard and flicked the electic kettle into life. Esther Marie was downstairs already attending to the fire. The two of them loved real fires. Delgatty bought sacks of coal from the people in the villages. The miners and retired miners had an allowance from the Coal Board and could never use it all.

He took her a mug of tea.

Jay, I would have got the tea. Let me cook you some breakfast.

I'm fine Marie. I'll get something later.

Well make sure you do. You're always forgetting to eat. You've been out for ages with the dogs. Everything all right?

He kissed her forehead and told her he had separated Rex and Queenie and they weren't very happy about it, especially Rex.

Oh how appropriate!

She picked her book up from the armchair and showed it to him; *Men and Gods* by Rex Carter.

I was reading Pyramus and Thisbe *only last night. Look.*

Oh God I remember that from school. I must've been eleven when I read it. Isn't that where They worshipped Heaven and now they must themselves be worshipped *comes from?*

Yes Baucis and Philemon. *But that's another story in the collection. The one that reminds us of Phyllis and Luke.*

Of course.

He took the paperback from her and skimmed the episode where the lovers Pyramus and Thisbe are kept apart by a wall with a chink in it and, despite its tragic conclusion, he smiled.

You keeping your hand in?

Esther Marie taught classics at the local comprehensive; one of a decreasing band of teachers in that subject as the new, more vocational curriculum came on the educational scene. It was a new school and about half the kids were bused in from surrounding villages; the rest walked or cycled in. They were nearly all the well-behaved sons and daughters of miners and a delight to teach according to Esther Marie.

I do so miss the kids Jay. The head has been very kind letting me have this time off but I really must get back next term.

Plenty of time. Easter's late April this year isn't it? Just make sure you are completely ready. Maybe leave it till September.

No I must go back in May.

Ah May! The bullfights in Madrid. We really must go this year. I haven't been since 1972, was it? I dreamt I was there last night and in the ring with the flaming bull!

I don't want to go again Jay. It's a cruel sport.

Not sport. Art.

It's a blood sport. Don't kid yourself.

Worse things happen in slaughter houses every day of the week. If I were a bull I'd take the arena every time.

The phone rang. Delgatty took it in the kitchen and caught it after six or seven rings. It was on the window sill and he could see the empty road through the louvre blinds as he spoke.

Oh hello. Yes a little out of breath Father. The cigars? I bet you're right.

The priest and Delgatty had first got to know each other twelve or so years earlier when Delgatty was playing rugby for his Church of England grammar school and Father Ryan was coaching their main Roman Catholic opposition. Ryan, besides teaching Latin on a sabbatical from his parish in Ireland, had been a scout for some of the senior Birmingham sides and had often spoken to Delgatty about trialling for maybe even county level. A broken leg at the age of eighteen had put paid to those plans and by the time he was fully recovered, a year later, Delgatty was on the verge of getting married.

He returned to Esther Marie.

It was Father Ryan. Says I ought to get down to Perry Barr tonight. There's a dog running in the third…

That's fine Jay but you've hardly any money. I thought you wanted to wait till Queenie was running again. The pups will be running soon too.

I said I'd put some money on for the Father. He's in Ireland and not coming over. Anyway I'll have to go.

Esther Marie was happy for Delgatty to go but she knew he was impulsive and naïve at times. He was a man of a generous spirit certainly but he was vulnerable to risk-taking, particularly when money was short, and she would rather he stayed at home.

Marie my Darling let me worry about the money.

She knew he was going to Perry Barr but she tried once more.

You can't drive. You're still banned.

Dexter will take me to the station.

3.

Dexter lived on the edge of Creswell, the next village. He had never worked down the pit himself but his father Zak had and the two of them shared, with Dexter's mother Elizabeth, sister Alice, nephew Mark and three greyhounds, a semi-detached, pre-fabricated house built by the NCB for their workers in the 1950's. The houses were supposed to have been a temporary solution to an accommodation crisis in the village but the small estate was still fully occupied over twenty years later.

Although the frail Zak was retired he had taken a great interest in the strike of 1972 and supported the miners in his small way by supplying tinned food and packets of tea from his larder. He did the same for the strikers of 1974. The latter strike had ended only the previous month when the Heath government had been thrown out on its ear.

Heath thought Thorpe and 'is Liberals would join 'im but Thorpe wasn't 'avin' any o' that. Liberals turnin' Tory? That day'll never come. They might be woolly-minded but theer not bloody daft, Siree.

Joe Gormley's a very reasonable man Delgatty. This should've been settled wi'out a strike. Heath got public mad wi' that three day week of hizzen and they wanted an end on it. That's why he lost, Siree.

When Delgatty had first moved to Derbyshire in 1970, he had thought people were saying *Surry* or *Sorry* at the end of their sentences but it was actually *Siree* as in *Sire* or *Sirrah* as a mark of respect.

Dexter was lacing his shoes.

Gormley's a bloody Tory Dad. Wait till Arthur Scargill takes over.

He pronounced *over* as in *hover*.

Then you'll see some proper action.

Scargill? He's trouble that one. Tha'll see what goes off if he gets in.

Can't wait Dad.

Delgatty would often call on Dexter in the early evening and enter without knocking. The dogs would leap all over the furniture at the sight of him and a few moments chaos would ensue until they calmed down. These were dogs who had finished with their racing careers with the exception of Pearl who had never had one. She was named after the Elkie Brookes' song because, like Pearl, she was a singer. Dexter had given this fussy creature only one handslip when she was about a year old. The bitch had shown no interest in the mechanical hare and, although it is quite a common phenomenon at this early stage in a greyhound's training, Dexter was so embarrassed that he vowed there and then never to take her back to the track. He was as good as his word and Pearl retired to whine on the settee before her racing career had even begun.

Delgatty loved to hear old Zak reminiscing about his days down the pit. He'd left Whitwell School at thirteen and in those days you either worked in the fields or in the mines. Zak's grandfather had helped sink Creswell pit around 1896 and his father had been there during the 1926 strike. It was natural for him to follow them.

Tha started ont pit top. Tha couldn't go downt pit till tha were fourteen any road. But soon as tha birthday come round that were it. Eleven bob a week in them days.

Zak recalled being sent by his father to join the Union at three pence a week and how the Union had represented him when he'd had his first problem with management.

We were supposed to fillt tubs wi' a fork to mek sure they weren't full o' dust. A supervisor, bend downers we called 'em, accused me o' fillin' a tub wi' a shovel and they inspectedt tub ont pit top. My union man came too and said there's note wrong wi'it. He was reight. Ah hadn't used a shovel.

He had hated the dark and the mice and rats. After his first few weeks underground opening doors for miners driving ponies through with their tubs, trapping it was called, Zak was given charge of his own pony.

Whenever Zak spoke of the pit ponies his old eyes glistened and he grinned toothlessly.

We used to bringt ponies up if they got injured or badly and a few came up duringt 'olidays. The first timet bosses said we were going ter bringt lot of 'em up fort summer closure it were bedlam Siree.

He described how the cages had to be adapted to hold the ponies one at a time and how the man in charge of a pony would drag it into the cage and have to crawl back out under its belly.

You could here 'em kickin' and shoutin' allt way up tut pit top. We used to tek their shoes off to mek 'em less dangerous, tha knows.

The pit would shut for a couple of weeks during the summer. Except for during the war, most miners and their families would pile on to the trains from Worksop to Cleethorpes. Those who hadn't would make an occasion of the release of the pit ponies from their underworld existence.

The ponies were backed out of the horse boxes into the field to stop them going berserk at the open space. They still charged exhuberantly around the field and a few appeared to panic. Some said it was the fact that they were blinded by the sunlight whilst others claimed they were establishing dominance in the herd.

There were fatalities amongst the ponies in the mayhem and people began to wonder about the wisdom of bringing them to the surface. At first they would answer to their names but over the two weeks the animals grew more surly and distant.

They seemed to 'ave a sixth sense. They some'ow knew on that Sunday night they were goin' back dahnt next day.

Zak recalled one occasion when the ponies broke out into the village streets on the Sunday night before the pit reopened; the men chasing round after them in the pitch dark.

And they were buggers when we got 'em back down, Siree. They would kick theer 'arnesses off an' all sorts. In the end we stopped bringin' 'em up. They've all gone now anyroad. Bin gone ten year or more.

During the war Zak had been called upon to help teach the Bevin Boys some mining skills. These were conscripts into the forces originally but Ernest Bevin decided that a small percentage of those aged eighteen to twenty five should be redirected to working in the mines. They worked without the glory or esteem of their military brethren and many stayed long after the war, at first by compulsion and then by choice.

Poor buggers were like fish outa water. But they were good lads and knuckled dahn tha knows.

4.

Esther Marie had just finished feeding the dogs their mid-morning breakfast when she heard the heels of Harriet come crunching on the gravel around the side of the house to the kennels.

I've been ringing the bell for five minutes.

Oh sorry. I thought I heard your car Harri.

I'll break my bloody neck on your drive Esther one of these days. No don't shut the door. Let me have a look at them.

Harriet stormed into the kennel. She pretty well stormed everywhere.

Oh bless them. Aren't they all beautiful?

They are beautiful just like you dear Harri.

Esther Marie beamed at her and looked down to Harriet's gold-coloured shoes.

Harriet was Esther Marie's sister. She had three children and was the greatest advocate of the spiritual value of marriage. Ironically she'd married a philanderer. After much agonizing and fears for her children's futures, she'd divorced him and set herself up as a marriage guidance counsellor. She remained aloof from any other relationships with men. Indeed she claimed to be a new woman after bathing in the mystical waters near what was reputed to be Avalon, well Glastonbury anyway.

Her house was full. She had provided refuge for two women and four children who had been suffering at the hands of violent husbands and fathers. There had been much irate yelling and the banging on Harriet's door for a while but it had gradually subsided as the abandoned men, probably quite gladly, readjusted to single life. In fact this small commune had worked well as the women could each get time off when one or two of them would take charge of the kids for the evening.

Harriet had become a mystic and a confirmed believer in Tarot readings which had come as something of a surprise to other members of the Women's Institute who weren't supposed to dabble in what was labelled a pagan activity by the elders of the church. Quite a few did go round to her house for readings when all the kids were in bed and she courted more popularity than the rather less charismatic vicar.

Let me make you some tea.

Esther Dear let's have a glass of wine. Jay must have a bottle somewhere.

It's only eleven o'clock.

So? I prefer drinking in the morning to any other time of day. It's rather wicked.

Of course Harri.

They sat in front of the log fire with their glasses full of Delgatty's chilled Chablis.

Esther I've brought you a book. It's a new publication Psychology and Behaviour Change *by Marks. I thought you'd be interested. I've read a couple of papers by him on agoraphobia. I didn't know it means fear of the market place? Did you?*

Esther Marie took the book and thanked her sister.

Yes of course I did. People think it means fear of open spaces but I'm fine in open spaces. I'm really quite a lot better now Harri. I'm not really agoraphobic. I'm fine in the garden or in the paddocks, pottering about. And I've been on a couple of walks with Jay and the dogs. If I'm honest I just like being at home. It's crowds that make me panicky. Jay says we can manage for a while without me working. He will look after me till I'm properly better.

And where is he now?

Perry Barr dogs.

Exactly. Perry Barr dogs.

5.

Whenever two or three were gathered in Delgatty's name there were two or three opinions. Some might say he would destroy himself. Well if you want a job doing properly. Delgatty knew that people pigeon-holed him as a gambler but he had never regarded himself as such. He hated losing too much to be a gambler. No he was a speculator who did his homework and was always looking for an edge. Betting for Delgatty was more like playing chess than gambling.

These people who talked about him would have to admit he'd done better than any of them. After all he'd bought his own cottage with a couple of acres out of that win on Nijinsky. Nobody knew exactly how much but he had backed the Vincent O'Brien trained horse to win The Triple Crown; Two Thousand Guineas, Derby and St. Leger. It was a lot according to Father Ryan.

Enough anyway. Probably three or four grand.

Perry Barr had just resumed evening racing under lights after Ted Heath announced his three day week in December 1973 when the nation's television closed early to prevent the electricity grid from overloading. They had raced mornings or afternoons to avoid using the floodlights. In fact they were forbidden by Government command to use electricity for such a trivial activity.

Delgatty had attended an evening meeting, deep in the Black Country, at Cradley Heath before the miners' strike ended. Cradley claimed to have installed a gaslight system which was the envy of all other tracks in these difficult times.

Sure enough on entry it was clear that the light was poor and Delgatty could barely see the dogs parading in front of the stands. But just as the mechanical hare flashed past the traps the miracle of *gas* was fully exploited and the stadium was bathed in celestial light for the half a minute or so it took to run the race. Everyone laughed at Cradley's two fingers to the collapsing government.

Delgatty now stood on the edge of the dimly-lit cinder car park at Perry Barr and called a taxi.

Station.

His face burned through the brandy as he fingered the sharp stab in his diaphragm between two buttons of his waistcoat. It reminded him that he had not eaten all day.

Delgatty reflected that he was in the shit for cash. He had been there before but maybe not quite so deep.

He had travelled to the Birmingham track to back the dog the Father had told him about. His bets had been nodded on, that is to say no money had exchanged hands. A bookmaker, Laverman, whom Delgatty had last seen in his bullfight dream, knew him. He had known Delgatty first as a *face*. *Faces* are people bookmakers learn to recognise as potentially dangerous punters with a good strike-rate of winners. He had eventually got to know him sufficiently well to accept his cashless bets.

Four hundred and fifty pounds to one and a half Fiery Finola. With a ring.

With a ring was the way the bet was to be recorded by his clerk and meant that Delgatty had not paid his stake.

Laverman rubbed his chalked price of 3/1 and replaced it with 7/4. Prices can move quickly at the dogs.

There is honour at the track and it was rather impolite of Delgatty to be betting a hundred and fifty pounds when he only had about eight quid in his pocket at the time. Fifty of it was for Father Ryan.

In a way his luck was in and he was spared the ignominy of ducking out of the track. There was a bomb scare. It was only a couple of years since Bloody Sunday in Derry and these alerts were quite common in the Midlands.

Everyone please move calmly outside the buildings.

Delgatty didn't need to be invited twice. He walked calmly outside the buildings, through the gate and temporarily away from his debt.

6.

Harriet and Esther Marie had been discussing Delgatty. Harriet looked Esther Marie in the eyes.

He's not reliable Esther.

I'm not married to him Harri!

He's got a sort of Tarot history about him. He started off as The Fool. He just walked naively into that marriage. He became a part of someone else's life plan.

The Fool? There's a lot of wisdom in Shakespeare's fools Harri.

Yes fools can be wise certainly but The Tarot Fool is the sort of raw material before any enlightenment. Next he was like The Knight of Wands.

The Knight of Wands?

Yes another character in the Tarot pack. He's charismatic, popular but with crazy ideas. He's a tilter at windmills. And he says he's going to look after you Esther. Where will it all end?

That's too one-dimensional. Jay is far more complex than that. I feel so sorry Harri. He was way too young when he married that girl. He's not crazy. He's level-headed in the main.

She took a tissue from her sleeve and wiped her eyes.

He hardly ever sees the child. Not properly. He did see her just before he got banned from driving. He told me he drove to her school. It's a hundred miles. He waited outside in the car till the kiddies came out for playtime. He didn't speak to her or anything; just watched her play with her friends. Then he left and drove back here. I don't know why he told me. He just did.

That is sad Esther but you mustn't let it become your problem. Anyway he did see her last summer holiday. In Cambridge, he said, and they went on the river. And he spent a day with her just before Christmas. So it's not hopeless.

Right I've brought the cards. I think you need a reading.

Esther Marie had dried her eyes but now she was nervous. She'd never had a reading before.

Isn't it supposed to be pagan though?

Don't be ridiculous. It's perfectly fine. The vicar doesn't know but I've got my own group at the Women's Institute and even the vicar's wife came round for a reading last week.

She took a pack of cards from her handbag and held them aloft in some sort of gesture to the heavens or the spirit world which made Esther Marie laugh out loud. She put them back in her handbag.

If you're not going to take this seriously we might as well forget all about it right now.

Sorry Harri. I won't laugh again.

Harriet began the ritual offering of the cards again. Esther Marie laughed again.

Right that's it. I'm not in the mood now anyway. I've lost my connection. We'll try another time. Maybe tomorrow.

7.

Delgatty pulled a packet of cigars from his jacket. In the brief flare of the light he pictured Laverman's heavies looking along the bar for him and it dawning on them that they would have to wait for their money. It would only be a matter of waiting of course. For how long though?

He shook out the match and dropped it on the taxi floor. No good now that the race had looked between Fiery Finola and the hare. No good now blaming Father Ryan for the phone call suggesting he get his arse down to Birmingham to back this good thing.

Sure Delgatty I believe 'tis the only fuckin' trier in the race.

Who was to know the dog would get left six lengths and only be beaten a neck?

Delgatty leaned forward to the skin, bone and Brylcreem that was the driver.

How long do you reckon to get to New Street from here?

Ten, twelve minutes, depends on the traffic.

I've got a fiver says you can't do it in eight.

The man half turned and Delgatty caught his grin in the flashing neon of a furniture store. He switched on the interior light and both men checked their watches. Delgatty felt himself sink into the mock leather upholstery as the taxi accelerated. He turned to wipe the steam from the rear window but the stab in his guts pulled him sharply back to face the front. He closed his eyes against the dizziness and kept them closed until the car pulled over to stop. He opened one eye. The interior of the taxi was alternately lit yellow, blue, yellow, blue. He opened the other eye.

Clipboard in one hand, adjusting his peaked cap with the other, a black figure approached in slow motion through the flashing night. Delgatty felt himself at the centre of a fused pinball machine. Bong. Bong. Bong. They were going to be booked by Zebedee.

For crying out loud.

The driver was not pleased, *his living, his missus* etc. Delgatty swung his nearside door open and sprang into his full charm mode.

Sorry officer my fault entirely. Please don't blame the driver.

Something about his mother and a phone call and a train at half past ten. Delgatty never knew how he did it but he really was very persuasive even though people sort of appreciated it was probably all bullshit. After about two minutes the copper put his clipboard back under his arm, said he wouldn't hold them up any longer and wished them goodnight even.

The two strangers laughed all the way to the station. Delgatty took three quid off the driver and called it straight. He got down from the cab and crumpled the three notes into his hip pocket.

Outside the train hangar the rain was falling. An old newspaper, stained with vinegar and chip fat, wrapped itself round his feet.

Heath Decrees Three Day Week.

Does God know about this?

He tried three phones before finding one that worked.

The GPO vandalise more boxes than the bloody vandals.

The box smelled of piss and the rain blew through a broken pane. He dialled and waited looking at his watch. She finally answered.

Jay I was in bed. Where are you anyway?

Delgatty explained.

Are you coming home tonight?

No Marie. Last train's long gone anyway but there's racing at Wolverhampton tomorrow so I might as well stay at Tony's and see if he can lend me a few quid.

The dog didn't win then.

It wasn't a question.

Go back to bed. I'll phone you tomorrow.

You'll be seeing Mary I suppose.

He sighed.

Well yes she'll be there of course. It's OK Marie. You'll have to sort the dogs out in the morning.

Oh really. I thought I'd just ignore them.

Her rare lapse into sarcasm surprised him and made him apologise again.

Delgatty put his fingers on the rest for a moment and looked in the tarnished mirror, wiping the rain from his face. Twenty eight years, maybe approaching the middle of his life. He phoned Tony who answered the phone himself for once. Delgatty said he was coming over and Tony told him where the keys were.

Let yourself in. I'll see you in the morning.

The brandy was wearing off. Delgatty lit another cigar, circling the bare bulb with smoke.

He bought an *Evening Mail,* got a platform ticket with the change and took the ten thirty five to Wolverhampton. The journey was only about twenty five minutes. He walked the length of one carriage and, as he passed the compartments, he noted two priests with two large bags, two ladies getting in some last minute knitting and a young man alone with a paperback.

I'm so sorry.

A Chinese man was coming out of the lavatory.

No my fault sorry.

Delgatty followed the man he had collided with and dropped into an empty seat in the compartment where two more oriental gents were preparing to play cards. He immediately flicked to the sporting pages in his newspaper. Delgatty scanned the card for Wolverhampton. Nothing leapt off the page at him.

The card game was just starting up between the three Chinese guys. Delgatty rapidly made the calculation that, although all Chinese people are not gamblers, there was a good chance that these three card playing men were. He didn't have long before Wolverhampton so he began. He folded the paper elaborately so that they could see he was studying the race card. He sucked his teeth in concentration. He took out his pen and marked a horse with a bold ink circle. He smiled ostentatiously. He even gave a little chuckle. At first he had attracted only the odd glance from the players as they were after all concentrating on their game. Gradually they began to take more interest in Delgatty's theatricals until one of them spoke in the broadest Black Country accent.

Are you looking at tommorer's Wulvrampton card?

From then on it was fairly easy.

So this bloke, a mate of the travelling head lad, tells me to get a monkey on for him - five hundred quid.

We know what a munky is maite.

Delgatty looked like he had a monkey. The two hundred guinea leather coat open to reveal the two hundred guinea wool suit, the waistcoat and the hand-made shoes. The concealed hole in the sole.

He didn't usually resort to such deception but it amused him and he wanted to see if he could pull off this little piece of mischief. A few quid would be handy too.

One of them asked the name of the horse. Delgatty explained his difficulty. There was the owner who was expecting a good price. Then there was the lad who looked after the animal. This had all been carefully prepared and it was really only a matter of courtesy to put a few quid on for the lads and lasses in the yard.

They handed over a fiver each and Delgatty stared for the first time at the name of the horse he had circled in the newspaper. He wrote it on the back of his platform ticket and handed it to the man who had been dealing.

News From Thebes.

He got down from the train at Wolverhampton and went through the exit chatting to the two priests. The porter on the gate saluted all three without asking for tickets.

Nasty night Gentlemen.

God go with you.

8.

He found the keys under the geraniums. The stairs in the Georgian house were unlit and he groped his way to the basement. This was where Tony had his flat with Penelope and Mary. His mother had the rest of the building as a private hotel. The girls had been students of art ten years earlier and then they had met Tony. He had enchanted them from the beginning. When they saw the cellar and his paintings they resigned their college places the same week and had lived with him ever since. They thought they'd learn more.

Mary used oils and watercolours. Penelope was a textile artist. She was an artisan weaver of great skill and used to sell her stuff, too cheaply Tony claimed, at craft fairs around the Midlands. These days she had become reclusive.

Delgatty was about to turn the knob on the door when it opened and Mary switched on a light.

Tony told me you were coming. I waited up. Do you want a drink Jay my darling?

I'll have a drop of what you're having.

Keep your voice down my lovely. Tony's asleep and Penelope might be too, if she's not working. Brandy OK?

Fine.

Delgatty left Mary sleeping in the morning. He took a shower and dressed in the previous day's clothes. He made his way up to reception at ground level where Tony's mum was fiddling with a few papers. Delgatty kissed the doll-faced woman and tasted powder. The effects of seven children and three husbands lined her face. She stood back to look at the man.

It's weeks since we saw you Jay. He's been talking a lot about you. He'll be delighted to see you.

So where is the genius?

He's on the roof.

Of course he is. I wouldn't expect to find him anywhere else.

Up three lots of stairs and you'll see the ladder through the skylight.

A gust swept Delgatty's long hair as he emerged on to the red roof tiles. Tony was fixing a television aerial in the angle of two gables.

Bastard thing blew down. How are you Jay? *Hang on a minute.*

He gave the spanner another wrench.

That should hold long enough to see Coronation Street *off the air.*

The men's voices were swept across the rooftops by the wind. Wolverhampton flattened out below them. Tony wedged himself between the gables like a man walking up a well. He pulled a packet of *Sweet Virginia* from his shirt pocket and rolled a cigarette. He licked the paper's edge, lit the fag with a match and blew the smoke to the Wolverhampton clouds. He proffered the pouch to Delgatty.

No thanks I only smoke cigars these days.

Oh really. I stick to roll-ups. Mary keeps bringing this dope home and I smoke that now and again. It gives me peace. I sleep better.

God I haven't smoked weed since London. Remember when we went to that squat in Ladbroke Grove wasn't it? They were all spaced out. That guy in the turban. He just sat on a table in this bare room and he nodded when we asked if we could stay. Remember when we had that spliff and you spent three hours studying a map of The London Underground?

A very interesting document and a perfect example of how to provide uncluttered information to people in a hurry. It's a work of art all right.

I'm sure that's true. Anyway are you still seeing somebody about your anxiety thing?

They say I'm voluntary but you never know. I'm fucking harmless though, apparently. I go in from time to time for a couple of days, sometimes a week. I enjoy it. Nutters are very interesting. I've got a painting class. They paint some great stuff Jay.

I bet they do.

One of the doctors there says that electric shock therapy might be what I need.

Delgatty was unequivocal.

That's shit. It's like taking a stopped clock and throwing it against a wall. Sometimes it works and the clock goes. Sometimes it's totally knackered and never goes again. Is everybody mental Tony? Penny sleeps all day. Esther's agoraphobic. You're....well nobody knows what you are.

Tony laughed.

Everybody except you dear Jay. I think it would be rather exciting to be electrocuted. I'd be like McMurphy; light up like a pinball machine and pay out in silver dollars.

I think it was pay off *in silver dollars. Pay out is too English.*

Pedant. Anyway I'm Welsh, not English.

One Flew over the Cuckoo's Nest was one of the few books Delgatty had read since his college days and he had insisted Tony read it too. These days Delgatty found *The Greyhound Owner* and *The Sporting Life* sufficient for his literary diet and all he had time for, although he occasionally bought *Private Eye* to keep informed of the current political scandals.

A seagull flapped by. It caught Tony's attention.

Mary and I went to West Park a couple of weeks ago. We often go to feed the ducks. We take good bread you know with seeds in. We don't want to give the little fuckers a heart attack. Anyway when we get there the lake is frozen up to the shore and the ducks are swimming about fifty yards off the edge where the ice has melted.

You paint a lovely picture Tony.

Shut up. There's a point to this. So we start to chuck the bread to where the ducks are but it's too light and the wind takes it and drops it on the ice. We expect the ducks to get on to the ice but they don't. They're park ducks for fuck's sake and used to people but they won't get on the ice.

We've now chucked all the bread and decided that if the ducks are scared of us we should walk away. So we do. We look back and the birds still haven't approached the food. And then we see a seagull closing in. You know they come inland in winter.

Course I do.

And then another and another. Then there's about fifty of the buggers and they're those timid little seagulls that never land. They keep diving and scooping the bread from the ice.

So the ducks weren't afraid of you. They were afraid of the seagulls; of being dive-bombed.

Exactly. They knew they were coming. Very interesting isn't it? You can never be sure of another's thinking. The ducks knew something. They knew something we didn't. It was a circular thing. The seagulls were wary of us and the ducks of the seagulls.

The two men digested Tony's tale in silence for a minute or so as if the lesson had just been read in church.

How's the funeral prep. going?

Tony had a notebook permanently about him. Mostly he wrote down things he had overheard in a bar or on the bus. He also collected malapropisms. Most recently he had recorded someone who was hoping to achieve a number of goals *in one foul swoop*, a prize-winner being asked to *step forward and pick up his momentum*, a lady in the butchers on election day asking what all the *hoopla* was about and someone asking if there was *anything in the offering.*

In the same notebook Tony was also continually writing and re-writing his own funeral service.

Yes OK. I'm in no rush though Jay. Tiptoe through the Tulips *is a possibility for the opening hymn.*

What the Tiny Tim version?

Oh yes it's the best by far. And I'm pretty certain to have James Elroy Flecker's poem at some point.

Tony recited the entire poem by heart from the Wolverhampton rooftops.

I who am dead a thousand years,
And wrote this sweet archaic song,
Send you my words for messengers
The way I shall not pass along.

I care not if you bridge the seas,
Or ride secure in the cruel sky,
Or build consummate palaces
Of metal or of masonry.

But have you wine and music still,
And statues and a bright-eyed love,
And foolish thoughts of good and ill,
And prayers to them who sit above?

How shall we conquer? Like a wind
That falls at eve our fancies blow,
And old Maeonides the blind
Said it three thousand years ago,

O friend unseen, unborn, unknown,
Student of our sweet English tongue,
Read out my words at night, alone:
I was a poet, I was young.

Since I can never see your face,
And never shake you by the hand,
I send my soul through time and space
To greet you. You will understand.

Delgatty applauded with genuine appreciation but, to amuse his friend, wiped an imaginary tear from his eye.

Who's going to read it Tony?

Nobody is going to read it Dear Jay. You are going to learn it and deliver it.

Tony nodded his head at the ladder and they both went down.

The two men weaved back down several flights of stairs to the basement living room. An African Grey parrot squawked on its perch. The smell of the previous day's marijuana hovered in the air.

The wall was covered by a fifteen by ten foot unfinished canvas of Calvary. The crucified Christ was only etched in like God was just developing the idea. His scribbled face bore a remarkable resemblance to Mary's in orgasm.

Tony I need to borrow a few quid for a couple of weeks. Can you manage a hundred?

Although the two young men had never discussed the matter it seemed that Tony had private means, a wealthy, absent father some said, and he did not flinch.

I never like people owing me money, you know that Jay. It's not good for them or me. You know what that old wanker says in Hamlet.

Polonius.

Yeah him. But I tell you what Jay, I could employ you for a couple of hours for a hundred quid. Take your clothes off and play Jesus to my Francis Bacon. It's tax deductable.

Oh yeah as if you pay tax.

Oh but I do dear Jay. We have to keep Blighty on the tracks. I like paying tax.

Delgatty had first met Tony when they were in their late teens. Tony had joined The Merchant Navy straight from his Catholic boarding school when Delgatty was doing his A levels in Birmingham.

At the age of fifteen Tony had steered his ship and cargo through The Solent and around The Needles in a Force Eight. He was the only man on board who was not drunk and the allegory of the ship of fools had informed his entire philosophy ever since. He had a facsimile woodcut of a medieval cartoon on his cellar wall depicting the rudderless, directionless crew of the story.

They had actually played rugby against each other - Tony on Father Ryan's team - but it was politics that brought them together; politics of the left. Anyway Tony, who was a quick and accurate stand-off, hated sport and couldn't see the point of it.

Delgatty was CND and had proudly worn the black and white badge. Tony was more radical than Delgatty and The Campaign for

Nuclear Disarmament was too soft for him. He was a member of The Committee of One Hundred led by Bertrand Russell.

Ten o'clock on a Wednesday morning in March Delgatty stood naked with his arms outstretched, his head lolled gently to his chest and a crown of tarnished Christmas tinsel on his head.

As we are in birth so are we in death.

He adjusted the crown and felt his naked balls swing gently with the movement. He edged away from the parrot.

I don't like the way Polly is admiring my nuts.

Mary appeared through the curtain which divided her bed from the studio, lighting her first cigarette of the day. She was wearing one of Tony's collarless shirts. Her shirt rode up her naked skin as she kissed first Tony's cheek and then Delgatty's.

Suffer little Mary to come unto me.

Tony sucked contemplatively at the end of his brush.

I wonder if I should paint Him with a Hard on.

He said both words with a capital H.

Delgatty dropped his arms and put them around Mary's shoulders.

That nasty man has been neglecting you hasn't he? He thinks more of that rotten looney bin than he does of you.

Mary looked at this religious icon with pursed lips.

Put your clothes on Jay. You're getting to me dormant passions.

Is Penny still abed?

Mary laughed and jerked her thumb at where Penelope presumably still slept behind the velvet curtain which defined her bedroom; red opulence in the Spartan cellar.

O yes she's abed all right, Shakespeare. She's working on a commission and is sewing pretty much all night in her room. She's such a perfectionist she keeps unravelling the damn thing and starting again. I thought you'd know about it. She's doing it for Harriet's church or WI or something.

Oh yes Harri said something about it.

She's probably still bye-byes. I'll get us some coffee

Mary disappeared through the door and they heard the soft tread of her naked feet on the bare stairs to the kitchen.

9.

Harriet pulled up on Delgatty's drive in her pale blue Mini Cooper. She eased her platform shoes on to the gravel and slammed the door shut, locking it on the handle with her key in one movement. She fished in her bag, produced a boxed pack of cards and held them up to the heavens and then rang the front door bell before entering the unlocked house. That would stop Esther Marie laughing.

Are you there Esther?

Esther Marie was on her knees and had just finished putting a match to the rolled newspapers under the logs in the grate.

Hello Harri dear. It's still cold isn't it even though it's Spring?

March is the cruellest month Esther.

Esther Marie smiled.

That well-known T.S. Eliot line. Right what's it to be? Coffee or something stronger?

Coffee is fine for me. I've brought the cards. Don't laugh.

To be honest Harri I feel a little down today and not at all like laughing. It gets like this sometimes.

Harriet embraced her sister.

You sit by the fire and I'll get the coffee. Is instant OK?

Harriet banged around in the kitchen filling the kettle and looking for mugs and the milk. They kept up a shouted conversation from room to room.

Where is Jay?

He stayed in Wolverhampton last night.

Oh at Tony's? Has Jay said anything about that WI banner Penny is supposed to be embroidering for me? I thought she'd have had it ready by now. We need it for Whitsun. I say Penny *like I know her. I've never met her. Have you?*

No. I think she's busy with her tapestry business. And no he didn't mention it.

We won't bother with the cards today Esther.

No let's have a go. It will divert me.

If you're sure.

I'll put up a card table.

The fire was flaming strongly when Harriet re-entered the room with the coffee. Esther Marie was sitting on a dining chair at the card table with its plush green baize and looked beautiful in the firelight. An empty chair opposite awaited Harriet.

Harriet chucked a couple of beer mats on the table and put the coffees down.

What's all this Tarot thing about then Harri?

Harriet explained the basics. She told her there were seventy eight cards and that the first twenty two cards formed the Major Arcana.

They're the cards representing high purpose and deep meaning. The other fifty six cards are divided into suits but instead of hearts and clubs and so on there are wands, cups, swords and pentacles. Each card has its own meaning but a group of cards together can interact and give a clear picture of a person's need to act or change maybe.

That must be Pentacleese *like in Greek.*

No it is pronounced Pentaculls.

And you are sure it's not a sin?

I'm ignoring that question. The cards tell a story in themselves. The Fool is the first card in the Major Arcana and he is a sort of Everyman, coming into the world from oblivion, travelling through the world getting lucky, getting unlucky. He begins by daydreaming his way through dangers he is blind to. That's why he reminds me so much of the young Jay. But he acquires knowledge and, most important, learns about himself. He passes through the world into Nirvana or Heaven. The story the Tarot tells reminds me very much of Bunyan's Pilgrim's Progress *or* Don Quixote *even.*

Shall we have a go then?

Harriet put her elbows on the table and shuffled the cards.

These cards are from America. They just published a Tarot deck with William Blake illustrations. What could be more Christian than that?

Yes but he was a primitive Christian Harri. He didn't hold with the Church or the clergy. He thought they did more harm than good. You remember the poem, The Garden of Love?

*I went to the Garden of Love
And saw what I had never seen:
A chapel was built in the midst
Where I used to play on the green.*

*And the gates of the chapel were shut
And* Thou Shalt Not *writ over the door
So I turned to the Garden of Love
That so many sweet flowers bore.*

The sisters spoke the final verse in chorus.

*And I saw it was filled with graves
And tombstones where flowers should be
And priests in black gowns were walking their rounds
And binding with briars my joys and desires.*

Dad taught us that poem when we were really quite little Harri.

Yes he did. Bless him.

Harriet continued to shuffle the cards, sometimes merging them upside down.

Whilst I'm shuffling I want you to think about what you want to learn from our session. Is there a particular question you want the answer to for example?

There's only one question for all of us isn't there?

Harriet nodded.

You mean, Is everything going to be all right? Yes. Of course. You better narrow it down a bit though. Let's just look at the year ahead.

Agree?

The year ahead then.

She divided the cards into three roughly equal piles and asked Esther Marie to choose the one she wanted her to use. She picked the middle one.

Keep thinking your question.

She placed seven cards one by one face-down in a V shape.

I hardly ever think about anything else Harri.

Right this is the first card.

She indicated the card at the left-hand top of the V.

And at the other side this card is the last one which will give us the outcome. The fourth one at the bottom of the V will suggest what is to be done. You ready?

Yes.

Harriet turned each of the cards over. The first card was The Devil.

O that's a great start! I told you it was wicked.

Esther it's not really the Devil. You can see he's half man and half goat. He's more like Pan the God of Nature. This first card represents the past and The Devil usually speaks of excess or even addiction. In your case it's more likely to mean too much restraint.

Look at the poor people in neck chains though.

Yes but the harnesses round their necks are big enough for them to slip off. They are chained by their own will. Their own excesses or their own temperance have taken them prisoner. Nobody else.

When all seven cards had been turned over the seven card spread read: The Devil, The Ten of Swords, The Hanged Man, The Knight of Wands, The Nine of Pentacles, The Queen of Cups and finally Death.

The last card represents the outcome Harri you said?

Yes.

And it's Death.

Yes but you're not sick or old Esther. The Death card is much more likely to signify change. Let's look at the spread as a whole and see what story it tells.

Harriet studied the spread earnestly for a few minutes before speaking. Her sister bit her lip to stifle a smile.

OK I have it. In the past dear Esther you have shown great love for your family and home but you have allowed yourself to be hampered by your own self-restraint. You have brought yourself down and The Ten of Swords, representing the present, says that you have suffered psychological wounds which reflect your lowest state.

You're sounding like a horoscope in Woman's Own.

The Hanged Man has you suspended like The Fool hanging upside down from a tree. You gain insight. Maybe you are gaining insight now. This is the beginning of your future and nothing can be the same.

Isn't every day the beginning of your future?

What is to be done? Well the next card The Knight of Wands is Jay, the charismatic and popular Jay. I told you about that card yesterday. The card suggests you should throw your lot in with him and he will see you through this change in your life.

The Nine of Pentacles is upside down and this is the only card in your spread which is a cause for concern. It suggests there is a harmful outside influence to your lives here and regrettably there will be a price to pay for your future success.

Esther Marie gripped her sister's hand.

That's a worry Harri.

Of course it's a worry. Life is scary. The Queen of Cups is you Esther. The home-maker, dreamy and mysterious but inclined to sadness.

Depression you mean?

No not depression but it could explain your agoraphobia.

Mild agoraphobia.

And the last card, Death, emphasises that all is about to change and change for the better. You've got to sacrifice the old way of doing things and find new solutions.

The two of them sat in silence for a while.

Harriet spoke first.

I need a drink.

Me too.

10.

Things were on the up. Delgatty had over a hundred quid on his hip and a day at the races ahead. His guts seemed quiet. He had remembered to eat. Mary had made him a bacon sandwich. He lit a cigar and turned to the day's major handicap in *The Sporting Life*. If he could make any sense of it this sixteen runner event would provide the value of the day. They would be betting at least 5/1 the field. He'd only been able to eliminate three horses as having no chance and that only because it had been pissing down all morning and the going would be a bog. This trio, he had decided, wouldn't act on this type of surface.

The taxi swung on to the slope leading down to the Tattersall's entrance. He got down from the cab and paid the fare. He added a tip.

Thanks Mate.

There was a small group of men at the top of the slope with fistfuls of notes playing *Find the Lady*. The dealer would move three cards around, one of which was a red queen and the others nondescript cards. Most of the players would in fact be decoys and belong to the house. It always amazed Delgatty that anyone would get involved in this obvious confidence trick. He stopped to watch. What usually happened was that when the dealer had shuffled the three cards and thrown them face-down on an improvised table, maybe a wooden crate, somebody had twenty quid on the Queen of Hearts and won. This was a bit of corn from an insider to encourage others to get involved. And sure enough the fools, without a hope in hell, did join in.

Delgatty was interested to see a new twist in this particular game. The dealer, in spite of displaying the usual, amazing dexterity clumsily dropped a card face-up on the ground. It was the nine of spades. Whilst he stooped to pick it up someone turned over the other two cards on the crate, identified the queen by bending the corner and turned the two cards back face-down. As the man stood up he found just about everyone in the huddle was holding a note over the card they all knew to be the queen. He turned it over. It was the nine of spades; the Death card as Dexter's mother Elizabeth always said when they were playing Brag in the club. Delgatty admired the dealer's sleight of hand.

The lookout whistled the approach of a copper and the whole assembly melted away.

As he was about to enter the track he heard his name called. It was Cadman and, although he made his living by selling tips and general dealings in the black economy, he did so with such panache Delgatty always called him Mr. Cadman. Cadman even had his own business card with the wonderfully erudite words *Mr. T. Cadman, Equine and Canine Speculator.*

There were a few of these tipsters doing the racecourse rounds. One of the most famous in The Midlands was Shocker who got his name from his wares, well before Delgatty's time. He used to sell tips for a bob written on a scrap of paper and sealed in an envelope. They were known as the Shilling Shocker. These days Shocker was conning ten bobs out of the punters. He blamed the inflation of 1971.

Cadman and Shocker didn't get on. The latter was a complete scruff and he had been ignored by the racing authorities as unworthy of their attention, despite his hanging around the racecourse bars cadging drinks.

Cadman on the other hand was always smartly turned out in his massive overcoat and trilby in the winter and his cream suit and panama in the summer. He wasn't allowed on the track having been warned off years before for some alleged offence ; consorting with a person or persons liable to bring racing into disrepute. That was a laugh for a start. Anyway he stood just up the slope from the gate.

Cadman's finest moment was when the car in which he was a passenger got stranded in the West Country half an hour before the horses went to the post for the two thirty at Taunton. He popped into a local fishmonger to use the phone and get himself a couple of quid on a horse he fancied. The fishmonger who had only ever had a bet in the Grand National became interested. Cadman gave him the name of the animal with the advice that it could not possibly get beaten. Exit the fishmonger to some local bookie up a lane in a shed. That's how you had to bet in the fifties when millions of bobs and tanners must have been lost amidst the creosote.

Cadman had spent the rest of the day in the local, waiting for the five o'clock back to Birmingham but called in at the fishmongers on his way to the station. Old Fishie was beaming from gill to gill. He slapped a whacking great white fiver in Cadman's palm and half a fresh salmon into a large white parcel. As Cadman was about to stagger out of the shop, stagger that is with the weight of the fish and twelve large scotch from *The Holy Cow,* Fishie wrote his phone number in indelible pencil on the wrapping.

Let me know next time.

Unfortunately whenever Cadman told this story, which was fundamentalist gospel in the Midlands' racing community, he could not remember the name of the horse or at what price it obliged.

Over the following few months Cadman supplied a string of winning tips - seven on the trot according to oral tradition and Fishie bunged him many a fiver through the post. But Fishie's bookmaker was not a happy man and the plug was close to being pulled on the golden reservoir. So Cadman reassured him that he would provide him with a loser just for goodwill. For the only time in his life Cadman sat at the bar in his Birmingham local studying *The Sporting Life* with a view to finding a loser. It was not so easy as one might think but he did it. Unfortunately he had set a trend and when he next visited the West Country, Fishie's premises had changed hands and locals in *The Holy Cow* said he had gone bust.

Over the years Cadman's sight had deteriorated and these days he was practically blind although many of the more cynical racegoers thought his white stick a con.

Got a winner for me then Mr. Cadman?

Only one Delgatty.

Go on then, I'll stand for it.

Delgatty took out a fiver.

Cadman caught his arm and took him aside.

Don't give me nothing Delgatty. This ain't a guess. You got readies?

His marbled eyes were bright in his soft piggy face.

This is fucking right Delgatty. I've not give it the mugs. The owner is a bookie only the horse isn't in his name. It's in his wife's maiden name Claudia something. It's an SP job so there won't be a penny at the track apart from ours.

Sometimes gambling coups are executed by not betting at the track thus allowing the price of a horse to get bigger. This way relatively small amounts of money in a large number of betting shops could reap high rewards via the starting price or SP. Cadman felt deftly under his heavy overcoat. The rain ran from the brim of his trilby down the raincoat of this old mountain. He handed Delgatty his stick and pulled out a tight roll held by a rubber band.

There's four hundred there Delgatty. You'll get at least tens. I trust you Delgatty. You know I can't go in meself.

Delgatty took the bundle.

I'll get you on Mr. Cadman and I'll see you here after racing or if I miss you I'll be in The Fleece *tonight. What am I backing?*

News From Thebes.

Delgatty entered the track with Cadman's roll stuffed and zipped inside his coat pocket. News From Thebes. He had to smile at the irony of it all. Perhaps it was an omen. No he didn't even want to think it.

He bought a *Timeform* racecard, something he hardly ever did but he wanted some sort of confirmation that News From Thebes had a chance. The comments were not encouraging.

News From Thebes:

A good looking individual who showed great promise at two and three years winning five races between five furlongs and one mile on Good and Good to Soft ground. He has not won for over a year now and seems to have lost his enthusiasm, veering badly under pressure in his most recent outing over ten furlongs. Wears blinkers for the first time today and returns to a mile having been considerably stepped up in trip in recent outings.

Delgatty walked through the arch into Tattersall's betting ring. The horses on their way to the post for the seller were cutting in almost fetlock deep; the silks sucked to the jockeys by the rain. He climbed the steps to the bar at the back of the stand with a decision to make.

Brandy, large one please.

Could he lay Cadman's bet himself? He scoffed at his own stupid notion.

Sure and pay him out next time I get a Triple Crown winner.

He could get Cadman's money on and weigh in with a hundred of his own. A fishy smell came over him.

The commentary echoed meaninglessly outside and the divots flew behind the small, coloured group entering the straight.

Favourite's lagged in.

Judge was watching from behind Delgatty's shoulder.

How are you Delgatty?

Judge, Judge, I'm good, fine yes. You were in my dream the other night. You were a picador.

Really. Backed that. Seventy to forty.

Yes really.

Judge was never particularly interested in anything unconnected to racing, though his sporting knowledge was vast.

And Mary, Esther Marie and Harriet were banderilleros or is it banderilleras?

He emphasised Harriet's name as he knew Judge carried a torch for her and he thought it might raise his interest in the topic. Harriet had absolutely no interest in Judge.

No not banderilleras. Those are the darts. Women have only just been allowed back in the bullring. Been banned since the 1930's so the timing of your dream can't be faulted.

You amaze me Judge.

Judge swung his field glasses down into his hand and coughed, a little embarrassed at being such a trainspotter. A delicate hand covered his mouth.

Judge was not on the legal circuit but was thus known because of his prowess at assessing a horse's or a dog's capability on the simple basis of conformation. He would delete at least half the animals in any race on this basis with a slash of his Bic every bit as though he were consigning them to jail. If he ended up with only one or two in a race he would have a bet but only if he thought there was value in the price.

What's your idea of the winner of the handicap Judge?

Which one?

The feature handicap.

Don't know.

None of us knows. What's your best guess or, put it another way, would you give News From Thebes a chance?

You must be joking. Good sort all right but it's the biggest dodge in the game. He wouldn't go on if his life depended on it.

Judge had a point. The horse these days did not seem to want to put his head in front.

Delgatty decided to confide in Judge, at least in part.

Judge I've heard that this horse is expected today. The source is reliable believe me.

He handed him a small blue bundle.

Get this hundred on for me but wait till late. I think the price is going to drift.

Judge stuffed the money in his pocket.

It's your money.

Judge, whose real name, someone once told Delgatty, was Percy had had an unhappy life and one could forgive his moroseness. His grandfather, the town's mayor, had seriously disapproved of his mother's relationships with men and did all he could to make sure she stayed at home. She was a strong and vivacious woman however and on a rare outing she met a beautiful man, fell for him instantly and the result was Percy. When Percy was born his grandfather believed he would bring bad luck on the family. He avoided Percy at all costs. He tolerated him in his early years but when he left home for university he gave him a grand in cash and told him he never wanted to see him again.

At the end of his first year Judge was invited to play for a select universities side at The Staffordshire Cricket Festival. He had had no contact with his grandfather but frequently phoned his mother. He told her of his selection for the team.

How odd. Dad is planning to go to the Festival. I won't tell him you'll be there. It will be a surprise and you never know it might just give you some common ground for a reconciliation. He loves his cricket.

Judge opened the batting that day and on only his second ball he went down on one knee to send a massive hook crashing into the members' enclosure. As the applause died down around the ground there was a rush of silent activity on the steps of the pavilion. In short, an old man had been struck by the ball and instantly killed. It was his grandfather.

Percy and his mother were left no money from the mayor's estate but he still had most of the thousand pounds. Percy did not return to university and had lived on his wits ever since. He determined to show that he was not the embodiment of bad luck and became a professional gambler to prove the point.

Delgatty liked Judge most of the time but his pessimism and monosyllabic responses got him down and he wouldn't actually seek his company. The two men had their own agendas and they couldn't really be called friends. Racing however was a culture that few understood and they were united in this one sphere.

The racecourse clock over the number boards showed four o'clock and the race was off at quarter past. The two men made their way to the paddock but were stopped en route by Cyril Laverman. Delgatty had hoped that this bookmaker who only usually bet at the dogs would not fancy a day at the races. Delgatty was the first to speak.

Mr. Laverman I'm sorry I had to dash last night. I looked for you but that bomb scare…..I'll settle up with you Saturday night. One and a half wasn't it? Are you standing here or just having a day off?

Both men knew that Delgatty had behaved badly but there were customer relations to consider. Delgatty was a well known face amongst the bookmaking fraternity. His Nijinsky win had attracted a lot of attention but, that aside, he was successful generally as a punter. He did have his losing runs however and always paid in the end.

Nah I'm just having a day out.

Fancy anything?

Nah. Poor card really. Very tricky. You?

Nah.

OK Delgatty see you Saturday.

His eyes widened as he said it.

Yes I'm pretty sure I'll be there on Saturday Mr. Laverman. Where else do you stand? Brownhills I know.

King's Heath, Hall Green. Here take this card. You can stick a cheque in the post.

He handed Delgatty a small white business card.

News From Thebes was walking round the paddock as quietly as you like. Inside his head anything could be going on. Delgatty inclined over the white paddock rail swinging his legs quasi-gymnastically, scuffing the soles of his hand-made shoes in the gravel.

It looks well enough but will he have it?

Judge looked at his notes, copious pencil notes on sheets of lined foolscap.

There's a line of form here Delgatty that would have this horse thrown in. It's a long time ago but it was on this ground in The Vernons at Haydock. He ran in that as a two year old, getting loads of weight but he was only beaten four lengths. Bloody good effort that. On that evidence you'd have to think he didn't train on. Either that or they've been pulling its head off for two seasons. The other thing is they've probably been running him over the wrong trip. He looks an out and out miler to me.

The jockeys filed into the paddock, two or three slapping their boots with their whips.

There were no connections with News From Thebes, no trainer, no owners, just the travelling head lad and the apprentice jockey who was to have the leg up.

This kid any good?

Judge shrugged.

Never heard of him. He claims seven pounds that's all I know. Probably his first fucking ride.

Great.

The ground had cut up quite badly and the turf was steaming in a sudden burst of early spring sunshine. The horse moved well to post and the kid let him stride out at a sensible pace without fighting him. Delgatty was starting to get quite a good feel about the whole thing.

Delgatty walked into the betting ring. The favourite was as he had expected around 5/1 and several horses were offered at 7/1 and 8/1. Fortunately there was quite a lot of activity concerning half a dozen horses and the market was strong. News From Thebes was generally 16/1. He felt his heart banging. If there was to be money at the track this price could disappear in seconds. If Cadman was right and this was an SP job then there would be no money at the track and the price could double. As 20/1 began to appear Delgatty decided to play safe and mouthed across the row of bookmakers to Judge.

Take it.

Delgatty stepped in and handed over four fivers.

Twenty score.

Four hundred to twenty News From Thebes. Ticket 347.

The bookmaker confirmed the bet, simultaneously rubbing the chalked 20/1 from his board and writing 14/1 in its place.

There was still a lot of money to get on and Delgatty had to move quickly. The 20/1 soon disappeared and he found himself betting five hundred pounds to thirty.

Monkey to thirty quid. Ticket number 46.

Four hundred to twenty eight.

He scribbled his bets on the back of the tickets. Some bookmakers didn't give him a ticket because they knew him.

Four hundred to forty. Down to Dogs.

Delgatty recorded these bets on his racecard.

It was now difficult to find even 8/1. The last 10/1 had been snapped up in front of Delgatty's nose by an athletic Chinese.

O shit no!

No time to worry about that now.

The runners are going behind the stalls.

The racecourse commentator made the announcement in an alien public school accent.

Although the betting ring is a coarse transactional market it is also a subtle place and the atmosphere can change for those with the antennae to sense it. It had changed now. There was shouting and whistling. The white-gloved panic of the tic-tacs confirmed that News From Thebes was the one to be on.

Delgatty had placed only about three hundred of Cadman's four hundred. He had to get the rest on in one bet. He strode over to the rails where the big firms are represented. Prices are not displayed and Delgatty asked about a couple of others horses before naming News From Thebes as of possible interest to him.

He's 10/1 with us Sir.

Lay me a thousand to one.

I'll lay you eight hundred to one hundred Sir. He's a big loser for us.

Delgatty had to accept these reduced odds at this late stage. He handed over the hundred quid, noted the bookmaker's stand name and joined Judge in the stands.

What price did you get Judge?

Twenties, sixteens, twelves. Those Chinese guys were all over the fucking place!

I know.

A single mile stood between News From Thebes and the winning post. One mile between one thing and another. It was soon over. He flew the stalls under his young rider and was entering the straight as the other runners were leaving the outskirts of Wolverhampton. Fully three furlongs from home the kid was looking round for any trace of the opposition. He cruised to an effortless victory without breaking out of a canter.

Did you ever see anything like that Judge?

No.

Delgatty sat down on the steps, instinctively hitching his trousers at the knee. He did some quick arithmetic and spoke aloud to himself.

The tax is over two hundred quid.

They went into the ring to draw. First to the rails where Delgatty collected the eight hundred odd quid after the Exchequer had taken its cut. He put the money from each bookmaker in different pockets. He kept the total in his head; it was nearly five grand. At the bar door Judge caught up with him.

You forgotten this Delgatty?

Do you know I had!

Judge handed over fifteen hundred quid and a few bits. A hand touched Delgatty's shoulder.

And we're griteful too mite.

The Chinese card dealer from the train pressed what turned out to be another couple of hundred into Delgatty's palm. They'd fucked the price but you couldn't fault their manners.

The feature handicap of the day had as usual been in the middle of the afternoon and there were three races remaining. Delgatty returned to the bar for a quick brandy before going to see if Cadman was still on his slope. Laverman was at the bar with a furious look on him, his hands shaking as he lit a cigar with a lighter. Delgatty took his drink to a barstool in the corner of the room and assumed the pose of one studying the racecard.

When Delgatty looked up from his card Laverman was in conversation with Judge. They stood toe to toe, the brims of their hats touching. Laverman's heavies stood close too, looking round the bar. No drinks for either of them. They were on duty.

After a couple of minutes Laverman span round, his Maigret white mac spinning around with him, and left the bar in a dash. He left the track in similar fashion.

What was that about?

Judge moved closer to Delgatty.

He's just pissed off about the price of that thing that just won. He was expecting 20's and it's returned 15/2.

You didn't say anything about our part in it Judge?

Didn't need to. He could see us all over the fucking ring.

There was no point in discussing it further. The two men didn't emerge from the bar until after the fifth race when Delgatty set off to find Cadman. It would be better to hand over the cash in the calm before the exodus after the final race. A small queue of early-leavers had formed at the Tattersall's exit turnstile and men in caps and coats and a couple of fur-coated women with foxes round their necks kept up a light Black Country banter at the delay.

Come on. Me woife's 'aving a boiby. I just mide me moind up.

A few minutes of this and the small group became more restless until word got through from the gateman that there had been an accident outside and a new tolerance took over. The spring air was filled with the sudden shock of an ambulance bell and as it faded the queue steadily poured through the gates as if following the diminishing sound.

Delgatty looked for Cadman. He saw someone he vaguely knew.

You looking for Cadman mate?

Yes.

No good looking here. He's in that fucking ambulance. This van hit him. Just standing talking to him and this fucking van flies up, hits him, nearly hits me and fucks straight off.

A copper walked over.

You ready now sir?

And the chief witness climbed into the cop car.

11.

Delgatty decided to walk into town. He had thought he would eat at an Indian in the centre but he'd lost his appetite. He sat in *The Molineux* for an hour and drank a couple of brandies.

It was time to get news of Cadman. He walked the few hundred yards to the *Fleece* and shook the rain off himself in the doorway.

Sid the barman had already seen Delgatty enter and was holding a glass under the brandy bottle. He paused to let the optic refill and looked at Delgatty with grey water eyes.

Sorry Delgatty.

About Mr. Cadman you mean?

Punch's over there. He'll tell you.

Delgatty pushed his way through the bar to Punch who was in one of the alcoves.

Poor old bastard. Coppers said he just walked straight in front of a fucking Transit. He's had it Delgatty. Finished, know what I mean?

What Mr. Cadman's dead?

Might as well be. He's seventy so he's not going to get over being hit by a fucking van.

Have you been to the hospital Punch? Would they let me see him?

They let me in.

Punch picked up his coke.

Do you want to come back with me Punch?

He shook his head. Delgatty sat with the boxer for a while, mostly in silence. Thomas Cromwell is reputed to have said that there are many kinds of silence. This was a weighty one. A silence heavy with the absence of Punch's mentor, Cadman.

Cadman had always declared that the best bet a man could have was one on one, if the odds were right. One man fighting another or playing snooker or tennis was the optimum betting situation for

Cadman.

Punch was, at thirty three, nearing the end of his boxing career when he was offered a thousand quid to throw a fight he was expected to win. It is generally assumed by the public that this sort of fixing is rife in the sport but this was the first time anyone had suggested such a thing to the teetotal, gentle man that was Punch. He fought under his real name Peter Royal.

Cadman frequented the boxing halls and was a great fan of Punch who had confided his dilemma.

Well do you think you can beat this bloke?

Course I can.

And it is going to be your last fight?

Yip.

So who would be most upset if you won?

I don't know. My ringside guys and trainer and everyone would be fuckin' chuffed if I won. I don't know who's behind it. The promoter maybe?

Well there's your answer then. You play it straight and I'll give you two grand if you win.

And that is what happened. Punch won the fight by a knockout in the third round. Cadman cleaned up at the 5/2 on offer and duly paid Punch his two grand. It was indeed Punch's last fight. No promoter would touch him afterwards. Some said Laverman was involved but they were probably just guessing.

They must know how he stands by now.

He got up, squeezed the boxer's massive hand and left the pub for the hospital.

The man at reception looked at Delgatty over his glasses. The hinges were sellotaped and the tape was brown with age. Delgatty, thinking that this man epitomised the run-down state hospital for which he was front-of-house, told him who he was and asked if he could see Cadman. The bloke in the specs ran his finger down a column of names in the scruffy ledger on his desk.

Mr. Terence Cadman.

He followed the porter's directions to the ward where the starchy sister met him at the entrance and took him aside. Delgatty introduced himself.

I'm afraid Mr. Delgatty there is little we can do other than to keep him comfortable. He's an old man and has serious internal injuries. There must be a strong possibility of pneumonia. From the shock.

She spoke in quiet Scottish.

Is he conscious?

Barely but you can see him if you wish.

Was it better to remember the old man as he was, standing up the slope at Wolverhampton?

OK.

He followed the crisp uniform down the tiled corridor in between the ghastly faces of the ill; nauseating journey through the sick underworld. Two patients were sitting on the bed of a third, playing cards and smoking cigarettes. Delgatty exchanged grimaces with them. He was touched by his own death. They arrived at the open door of a side ward and the sister stood back to let Delgatty enter.

Cadman's head and shoulders were slightly raised by the framework of the iron bed. A plastic bag of blood was suspended over him. The rattle of his efforts to breathe filled the room. He peered at his misty visitors.

Mr. Delgatty to see you Mr. Cadman.

Delgatty leaned over the old man.

Mr. Cadman. Stupid old bugger you are then.

Cadman smiled faintly and spoke softly into Delgatty's inclined ear.

Not so fuckin' stupid.

He narrowed his blind, glassy eyes and squeezed Delgatty's fingers.

You hooked one out there Mr. Cadman. I've brought the money. You could have private treatment.

Cadman shook his head.

I shan't be coming out of here. They've done for me Delgatty. Done me up like a kipper.

Delgatty nodded and smiled at the cliché.

And the police? Are they saying it was an accident?

No fuckin' accident. No fuckin' accident. I'm tired Delgatty.

He coughed and Delgatty heard the phlegm rise in his throat.

You keep the money but see Punch all right for a good few quid. I think you'll make it big with that behind you.

His puffy old eyes closed. Cadman was in a one to one battle now all right and the odds didn't favour him.

I'll keep it till you get out.

Tell me about the race.

Delgatty told him, sitting on the edge of the bed touching the floor with one foot and swinging the other.

He looked well, the horse did, and the rain stopped just before the race. We had a bit of 20's early on but you averaged about 12's to your money.

Cadman was asleep and rattling. Delgatty finished the story though, lightly caressed the old man's arm and left.

The next morning he phoned the hospital. Cadman was dead. Delgatty set off for home and Dexter met him at the station in Sheffield.

12.

Most weeks when Delgatty was at home he would wander down to Creswell village with Dexter and play snooker in one or other of the three working men's clubs. They played as a pair against all comers and took these games very seriously even though the sums of money involved were invariably small. There wasn't a lot of money about. Men were still recovering after the strike.

One quirk of their game was that Delgatty, who had learnt some Italian from a former girlfriend in Manchester, would always shout out his and his partner's break in Italian.

Venti Due, Dexter! Trenta Nove!

Dexter enjoyed this piece of nonsense but never so much as when either of them potted the blue and they would yell simultaneously.

Cinque!

Delgatty, who seldom swore, could never remember who actually started it but he and Dexter would swear at each other with a ludicrously exaggerated London accent; certainly exaggerated for Derbyshire. Thus if Dexter missed a relatively simple red, Delgatty would regale him.

Yoo facking baarstud!

When Delgatty fouled on the pink Dexter would erupt in southern style too.

Yoo facking cant!

As the evening and the drinking wore on they would each allow themselves to be completely taken over by this imaginary dialect and would conduct entire conversations whilst playing Whist.

Yoo gowing ter ply thet facking jeck or wot?

Nah Maite Oi'm gowing ter ply the facking aice.

And even as they left the club it would continue. They would walk to the edge of Creswell and maybe sit for a while on the bench put there for the old ones to watch the school kids playing sports. They would engage in the re-enacting of the old village story that was supposed to be true. Delgatty would step into the road and pull up in an imaginary lorry and shout to Dexter on the bench.

Oi John 'ow doo oi get ter Cackney?

Dexter would throw himself into his part in his normal dialect this time.

Ow did tha know my name were John?

Oi guessed.

Well guess thar fucking way to Cuckney!

Eventually the two would separate and Delgatty would start up the hill to where he lived on the edge of Bakestone Moor about half a mile away, just past the allotments. They would begin with slightly raised voices a hundred yards or so apart.

Yoo facking baarstud!

Yoo facking cant!

By the time they were half way to their houses each could still distinguish the other's yell.

Faaaacking baaaarrrstuud!

Faaaaackkking caaaannt!

As Delgatty reached his gate he would utter one final yell and wait to hear the quavering distant retort that meant Dexter was home.

Ffaaaa.kk..iii.....nn..cccaa...nnt!

13.

His licence had been returned through the post and Delgatty's motor was back on the road.

He drove down to Wolverhampton alone and went round to Joseph and Son, the funeral directors. On the internal door was a black plate with white printing.

Sympathy with Efficiency.

He stepped into the carpeted office holding an LP which Esther Marie had insisted on wrapping in brown paper.

There was unexpectedly plenty of light through the upper half of the leaded windows. He had only time to notice this and the smell of air freshener when an immaculately modern-suited man in his thirties emerged from behind a curtain at the rear of the room. He checked himself in the long mirror, straightening his collar and twisting his tie to centre it. Delgatty thought he had seen this man somewhere before.

Music began playing softly and Delgatty recognized it as Chopin.

Good morning Sir. How can I help you today?

Americanisms were establishing themselves in Wolverhampton.

I've come about Mr. Cadman.

Mr. Cadman?

The young man looked confused.

Mr. Terence Cadman? The hospital told me he is here. He's dead.

Son of Joseph, as Delgatty imagined he must be, flicked through some papers on the Habitat desk.

O yes Sir I do beg your pardon. He arrived last night. I've been off for a week. At a health farm. Is Mr. Cadman a loved one?

He was a friend.

Delgatty spoke with some emphasis. He had read Waugh's satire on the American way of death and wasn't going down that route.

A friend, I see.

Look can we fix things up? I should be somewhere else.

Delgatty grinned.

Of course. I'm Joseph Junior. My father is out at the moment but I can deal....

He proffered a brochure to Delgatty from a pile on the desk. He declined to take it and it hung limply from the outstretched arm of the undertaker. Delgatty felt a little sorry for him.

Look. I don't want to seem callous but don't ask me to choose coffins, handles, cars. You choose. Do your best.

Certainly Sir. Do you envisage burial or...?

Cremation.

Quite. Are you the designated next of kin?

No I'm the designated payer of the bill. He has no relatives as far as we're aware. What's a funeral cost?

Well..

Roughly.

About four hundred pounds.

OK spend five hundred if you need to. Where do I sign?

He dashed off a signature where Joseph indicated.

There'll only be half a dozen of us. We'll send flowers here. Put an ad in The Express and Star. *On the racing page would be good. More likely to be seen there.*

The young man glanced at himself in the mirror, flicked his tight, black curls and nodded. He consulted his desk diary, adding notes.

I see the police want the results of the post mortem before the ceremony can be conducted so it would be next Wednesday before the paperwork could be completed. Meaning Friday for the event.

OK. How soon could we have the ashes after the event?

The event. Delgatty could feel his irritation rising at these euphemisms.

There is a bit of a backlog Sir. What with all the industrial action. It will probably be another week after that.

When they're ready send them round to this address.

Delgatty wrote Tony's address on a pad on the desk.

We could keep them here for you, Sir.

O yes. That would be better.

Would you like to see Mr. Cadman , Sir?

Delgatty remembered the old man asleep at the hospital; the bruised, swollen face, the bag of blood and the plaster-of-Paris arm with the tube fixed to the wrist.

No. No. The others might. Would they come here?

Yes Sir. By prior appointment if possible.

Delgatty turned to go but turned again to face Joseph who dabbed at his forehead with a red spotted hanky and checked himself once more in the mirror.

They will be his ashes won't they?

O yes. Don't believe what you read in the colour supplements.

He tried to smile reassuringly and Delgatty reciprocated. His irritation under control he decided he quite liked this honest fop.

What's your first name Mr. Joseph?

Conrad. I'm sort of back to front.

I feel as though we have met before Conrad. You ever been to Madrid? The bullfights?

Good grief no. No never but you do look familiar.

Delgatty grinned and handed over his packet.

I nearly forgot. Please play this record during the ceremony. He gave it me after I got married.

He passed the parcel across the desk.

It's Sinatra's Love's Been Good to Me.

Conrad Joseph looked distastefully at the brown-papered object as he opened it. Delgatty hadn't thought Sinatra that bad though he preferred the Johnny Cash version.

Conrad, you seem a little distracted. Is there a problem?

No everything is fine. We'll have to clean it before we play it. The equipment is very expensive.

Delgatty's attention was drawn to a half life-size statuette in the corner of the room just inside the office door. It was a spindly old man wearing a straw hat and leaning on a crutch. He had a pet dog sitting at his feet.

Who's the old man Conrad?

That's Papa Legal. He's got the keys to the gate of Guinea.

Guinea?

Yes that's the spirit world. You can't go in without his permission. People in my culture usually make him a small gift. A few coins perhaps. He is particularly fond of a smoke though.

Delgatty pulled a cigar from his packet and rested it on the statuette.

There you go Papa Legal. Enjoy your smoke and look after Mr. Cadman for me.

The shop bell rang with a melodious irony. A most beautiful Japanese woman in her late twenties entered.

Darling this is Mr. Delgatty

She looked at the stranger and spoke his name.

Delgatty.

Mr. Delgatty this is my beautiful friend Yoko.

She spoke her own name.

Yoko.

14.

Dexter was the cock of the village. He was a peaceful man in the main but he could flare up in anger in an instant and you could believe he would be able to kill a man with one blow. He could probably even do Punch some damage. He stood about five foot ten but weighed around eighteen stone. People liked him but, let's just say, they were cautious of him.

Delgatty was not cautious of him and felt at complete ease in his company. Dexter liked Delgatty a lot although they did have their minor disagreements, mainly over the way one of them had played a hand of cards. He was impressed with the way Delgatty handled dogs and one dog in particular; Boffy's dog.

Boffy's dog was notorious in the village. Everyone was intimidated by it including Dexter. Sometimes it would lie for hours across the doorway of the grocers Lipton's and very few dared leave or enter, making a big dent in the shop's takings.

Nobody knew if the dog had actually bitten anyone but he was surly, menacing and unruly, having lacked meaningful discipline at any stage of his life. People often take on a dog without the slightest idea of how to handle it. And they can be deadly weapons.

Boffy, a miner and incidentally quite a good poker player, liked to take Mrs B. and the kids to Butlins when the pit shut for two weeks in the summer but no boarding kennels would take Boffy's dog. He'd been to all the local custodians and the dog was barred throughout the county.

One night, after a few drinks, Delgatty carelessly offered to look after Boffy's dog for a couple of weeks. There was a general expression of disbelief around the bar; not least from Dexter.

In the summer of 1971 Boffy's young lad - Boffy didn't trust himself to persuade the animal to leave Lipton's doorway let alone the village - put the dog on a lead and pointed it in the direction of Delgatty's cottage. It pulled him from Creswell to Bakestone Moor in record time for dog and boy.

Boffy's dog was more bull than dog, more lion-like than canine. In layman's terms he was a huge, insane, black Labrador cross. Very cross.

Delgatty met the pair at the gate and led them around to a temporary kennel he had created in an outhouse, well away from his own dogs. Ordinary dogs, although this was in no sense an ordinary dog, do not mix with greyhounds which are an elite and exclusive group of animals. It would be rather like introducing a fat person with a cold into the Olympic Village.

The boy managed to get the dog to the door of his new abode but it was Delgatty who made the dog's mind up for him and shoved him inside.

An hour later Delgatty took him the finest dog's dinner on God's earth. There was one pound of minced beef which he bought on a monthly basis from a supplier of cattle that had died of natural causes and was therefore unfit for the likes of us. There were two pounds of cooked vegetables and a loaf of slightly stale, brown bread courtesy of Lipton's with whom Delgatty also had a deal. In short it was a meal fit for a greyhound.

The dog was left in the kennel all night and made not a sound. The next day Delgatty gave him breakfast of a brown loaf and a pint of milk and let him off in the smaller of his two paddocks for most of the day. He wouldn't use that paddock for his dogs for a few weeks he had decided, in case of infection.

On the third day he put him on a lead and walked him for an hour after he had walked his own dogs. After that it was easy. Boffy's dog began to walk properly on the leash, to glow with health and had even started to smile. Boffy's lad immediately noticed the difference in the dog when he collected it.

Two years later Delgatty called on his mate.

Give us a hand to bag some coal up Deck will you?

Dexter was happy to give a hand and jumped in the old Vauxhall.

Where are we going?

Boffy's.

Thar jokin' ain't tha? I'm not getting aht't car till that fucker's locked up. I'm stoppin' ahtside gate any road.

Actually Delgatty himself was rather nervous opening Boffy's gate. It had been two years after all. He was especially anxious when he heard the bellow of the animal as it charged from the kitchen. It ran straight at Delgatty, leaping towards his face before finally placing its feet gently on his shoulders and greeting him with the harshest breath and broadest smile imaginable.

It was a wonderful moment and Boffy, Dexter and Mrs B. laughed when Delgatty declared that he had taken a thorn out of his foot once.

15.

Cadman's funeral was sparsely attended. There were no family as the solicitor dealing with the estate had not been able to trace any in the short time available to him. The estate wasn't much. The house Cadman and Punch shared was rented. Delgatty had given Punch the cash for the next year's rent out of Cadman's winnings and said, if he could, he would continue to pay it.

Delgatty and Punch helped carry the coffin with Conrad and a professional from the funeral parlour. Sinatra played from the church balcony.

I have been a rover
I have walked alone
Travelled every highway
Never found a home.

Conrad ran his hand automatically over his hair immediately he put his burden down and smiled self-consciously when he realised Delgatty was watching.

Delgatty had told Esther Marie and Harriet they didn't need to travel all the way to Wolverhampton for the funeral but they had wanted to be there even though they didn't know Cadman. They wanted to meet up with Mary, Tony and Penelope anyway and they thought it important to help swell the anticipated, small congregation.

Tony rarely missed the opportunity to attend a funeral. He had his notebook at the ready in case there were any nice touches he might include in the arrangements to mark his own death. Dexter and Judge made up the remainder of the party, the former in a flowery tie borrowed from Delgatty, the latter in black but then he always was. Judge, who hardly knew Cadman, was there because he hoped he might get to talk to Harriet.

At the last minute Penelope had said she might meet them later for a drink.

I'll introduce you to Conrad, Tony. He's a real live funeral director.

Which one is he?

He's the tall black guy with the afro hair.

He's beautiful.

He certainly is. And he knows it by the way.

The vicar was OK. It must be difficult delivering a meaningful service to such a small group. At least he didn't say anything about the funeral being a celebration of Cadman's life and he didn't say Cadman had been on a journey or any of that clichéd nonsense.

He spoke of the Holy Spirit and how he was like an interpreter at our shoulder articulating what we don't have the words to say for ourselves, negotiating on our behalf as it were. Delgatty thought that sounded right. He said the Holy Spirit was like the backing singer of the Trinity, like The Imperials on Elvis' *How Great Thou Art*, making the picture whole.

Then to prove the point, the vicar taking advantage of the undertakers' modern hi-fi system, played the whole of Elvis' version right there and then in the church. A few tears were shed. Even Judge felt his throat ache.

Delgatty thought Father Ryan would have appreciated this modern Anglican. Tony was fairly impressed too and put the service down as 7/10 in his notebook. Tony's assessments were always rather harsh.

16.

Delgatty picked up his bag and left the buffet bar. Walking down the corridor, he steadied himself against the walls to stop his drink from spilling. He knocked on a compartment where the blinds were drawn and the door slid open. He was greeted by Skinner.

Ah Delgatty we saw you at the station.

Skinner. How are you son?

Skinner banged the door closed and scratched his arm through his shirt sleeve. He'd had excruciating eczema since boyhood.

Skinner had essentially been a flapping man. Flapping isn't an illegal form of racing. It just has no official recognition and no authorising body. Individual tracks make their own rules and most are run just as efficiently and effectively as their NGRC counterparts. The NGRC did however look down on their members' participation in flapping and you could be warned off for running dogs under both set-ups. Nobody took much notice however.

Delgatty only used to see Skinner at the flapping tracks but recently, with the advent of Brownhills Stadium, it would be an understatement to say Skinner frequented the new venue. He haunted it. He never went racing anywhere else these days. He knew every dog that ran there and although he never seemed to have any proper money himself he would alert bookmakers to likely gambles and he made enough out of his advices to live on. He was, however, to most dog men a spoiler, an impediment to their hard-earned right to a price.

Everybody thought, no knew, Skinner to be a pain in the arse. Skinner probably even knew it himself.

Inside the carriage three men were playing Brag; a suitcase thrown across the seats as a table. A girl in her twenties sat against the window and, although she didn't turn on Delgatty's entrance, he knew she was watching him in the black of the speeding window. He felt he knew her from somewhere.

Father Ryan was one of the men. He picked some notes off the seat next to him and handed Delgatty the fifty quid he owed him from his losing bet at Perry Barr.

No Father. You keep that for the Sunday School.

Thank you Delgatty. It will be put to good use. Delgatty now. How am I going to introduce him to you?

Father Ryan took a slug from his hip flask before addressing the strangers in the compartment. The Father, although a little drunk, realised he was embarrassing his friend.

Let's just say he's a feller knows a dog when he sees one. Well Delgatty what takes you to Dublin? You're not running away from the bookmakers I hope. Sure I heard you left the track with a little bill the other night.

He spoke with clipped Irish vowels with a touch of humour but without admonishment.

Sheer forgetfulness Father. Oh and there was the bomb.

The three men laughed, Skinner, Ryan, the one Delgatty did not know and the girl he thought he knew. The compartment was thick with cigarette smoke and smelt of booze, farts and the girl's deodorant.

Let's open a window somebody.

Skinner pulled the clasps on the small central window and opened it.

He sat down opposite Delgatty and introduced him to the two strangers.

As the Father has said, this is Delgatty. That's Tom and that's his girl friend.

The young woman looked embarrassed at the title. The man Tom was thirty years older than her.

Diane, she's called.

Tom and the young woman herself corrected Skinner in unison.

Diana.

They're going to buy some dogs and I'm going to check them out. The dogs.

Good decision. You could do worse than get Skinner to cast an eye over a dog. Good decision.

Delgatty caught the Father's eye and they were thinking the same without articulating it. Skinner knew his dogs well enough but he wasn't great company, what with his persistent scratching and untidy eating habits.

Diana looked up from her book. Delgatty shook the two strangers by the hand. The girl lowered her eyes. He put his half-empty glass down on the suitcase and swung his bag on to the rack.

I could do a bit of negotiating for you if you like Delgatty. It's often better to have someone doing the donkey work for you, like.

Skinner, the perennial go-between, loved to be involved in one way or another. Father Ryan interrupted to save Delgatty responding.

And is it a dog you're after in the Green Country Delgatty?

You a dog man then Delgatty?

It was Tom speaking.

Yes I guess I am. Yes I'm a dog man.

I tell you Delgatty the whole fuckin' dog game's bent. Sorry Father. Last week I saw my sister at Aldershot, flappin'. We was in the same race. I says, What's your chance girl? *She says,* Stopped. So is mine, *I says. Hers won and mine was second. Fuckin'* Stopped, *she says. Me own fuckin' sister. The whole fuckin' world's bent. Sorry Father.*

He meant sorry for the swearing.

Father Ryan knew what Delgatty must be thinking and chipped in again.

What sort of a dog would you be after Delgatty. A top grader for Brownhills or what now?

A good dog Father. A dog for The Cup maybe.

Ah a good dog. They cost an awful lot of money.

Yes Father. What are we playing?

Tom stood up and pulled a new pack from the inside pocket of his jacket on the luggage rack. He broke the sellophane and shuffled the cards offering Father Ryan the stack to cut.

You're a Midlander, Delgatty.

Delgatty was surprised at this assertion. He knew he'd had quite a broad Wolverhampton accent as a kid but had thought his education had refined it into near extinction.

Yes I suppose I am. Yes I am. You've got me summed up Tom. I'm a Midland dog man.

Delgatty produced a thin green wad of about a hundred pounds. He had three grand with him and was prepared to pay around fifteen hundred for the right dog. He loathed banks and parsimonious bankers but had stuck the rest in a building society account the day after Cadman died. Building societies were supposed to be for the mutual benefit of all. Banks were to be avoided. They'd got everybody's money and they wanted to keep it one way or another. His father Luke had told him that a bank manager would rob you with a fountain pen.

You been 'avin' it off at the dogs Delgatty?

Tom grinned as he dealt the cards.

Pound in the kitty. Pound to go. Black two's floating. All right?

Black twos floating. All right.

The group responded positively except for Diana and the penniless Skinner who both signalled their disengagement. The girl returned to her book.

What are you reading Diana?

Oh just something for college. Herodotus, The Histories. *You know it?*

Delgatty didn't want to explain that he knew the book because Esther Marie taught it at A level.

Yes of course. I've never read it but I know of it. What college are you reading at?

Girton.

The women's college?

Yes. But there's talk of it becoming co-ed.

She said *co-ed* with heavy emphasis as though scoffing at the fuss such a radical move was causing in Academia.

She turned her head and looked back to the window.

Tom spoke to Delgatty.

You support The Wolves?

Nah I was always a Baggie. West Brom was my team.

Delgatty picked up his three cards and saw he only had a queen. He put them back face-down on the suitcase.

Shame about Astle. Finished his England career when he missed that goal in Mexico.

England's loss. He's still banging goals in for us.

Now you've moved up to Derbyshire do you watch Derby?

Nah Skinner. These days I sometimes watch Wednesday with my mate Dexter. He's a big fan. They're in trouble this season too.

When Sheffield Wednesday were at home Delgatty and Dexter would make a whole day of it, finishing up at Owlerton dogs for the evening, getting a curry on the way home and maybe getting into a late game of poker if one of the pubs in the village was having a lock-in. If you could survive the match, the dogs, the curry and the poker and finish a fiver in front, well that was something to celebrate.

Delgatty looked at his cards again as if to remind himself of some quality in his hand. The train shook through some points rattling the windows. Three one pound notes bounced pathetically on the suitcase.

The Father stacked. Tom threw in a pound. The girl in the corner yawned, swung her legs up under her and closed her eyes.

The two men threw in another couple of pounds.

What you got?

Queen, Tom.

Take it.

Father Ryan returned to the football.

United are in real trouble aren't they though?

All a bit long in the tooth now Father.

Tom tapped a *Peter Stuyvesant* out of the soft packet and offered them round the carriage. Skinner took one.

Posh fags Tom.

Nobody else did.

Best's not helping. It said in The Mirror *he missed training again last week.*

Skinner, a lover of conversation, was sitting forward, cigarette angled in his mouth and with hands clasped in front of him.

And there's this business with Miss World. She says he's nicked some jewellery or somethin'.

The priest didn't want to hear anything said against his hero George Best and he brought the conversation to a close.

Load o' bollocks. That'll be thrown out o' court. What sort of money you want to pay for a dog Delgatty?

The Father sorted his cards without looking up.

Don't talk so much Skinner. Delgatty is no man for the small talking in the middle of a game of cards. I'll go a fiver.

Delgatty knew he was bluffing. He had three spades in his own hand. The train, a thin line of light, crashed on through the blackness.

Delgatty won a few hands; nothing much. He stood up, stretching his arms to the ceiling of the compartment. He felt tired. The girl was asleep, swaying and nodding to the train's movements, and he envied her.

Gentlemen, I need a drink.

Tom offered him a can.

No thanks. A proper drink. A short.

He drew the door open inhaling the clean, smokeless, fartless air of the corridor.

I'll come with you.

The priest was on his feet waiting for Skinner to move the suitcase.

The two men swayed to the buffet car. Delgatty brought a brandy and a glass of Guinness to the table.

Sorry they've only got bottled. Did you hear about Mr. Cadman Father?

Yes I did. A terrible business. Poor old man.

Delgatty stared into his drink and Ryan stared at Delgatty.

You look tired Delgatty.

Yes.

How's your young daughter?

Delgatty frowned fleetingly and looked up. It pained him to speak of his absent child.

She was well enough when I saw her last. It was the day after her birthday. I went down to Cambridge and spent the afternoon with her. We went on the river. Nice sunny August afternoon.

Delgatty had been at Manchester University in 1968 on a local government grant of about four hundred quid. Phyllis and Luke had chipped in what they could afford and he managed OK, living in university accommodation.

Just before his first year exams he had broken his leg playing for the First XV and ended up in hospital for a couple of weeks. One of the nurses was Angela and the two of them fell in love. When Delgatty was back on his feet they spent illicit nights smuggling each other into their rooms either at University Hall or The Royal Infirmary.

That summer Angela became pregnant and a registry office wedding was hastily arranged in Birmingham. The stark occasion was witnessed only by Luke, Phyllis and Angela's parents. That night they stayed in a hotel together but the love they thought they shared was already dying. The next day Angela went home to Cambridge. Her parents said Delgatty could visit her when he wanted; stay overnight even.

At first he would write to her two or three times a week and she did respond more often than not. The letters grew more infrequent on both sides. That September Delgatty found a decent bedsit for the two of them in Manchester but she never came back to him. He knew she never would. He decided to resign from his Philosophy course and go home.

When the child was born Luke got a phone call from Angela's dad. He and Phyllis insisted on driving Delgatty to Cambridge to see his baby daughter. He'd seen her maybe four or five times since.

And how old is she now?

She'll be nine in April this year. God Father, it's all been such a mess. Funny thing is I'm still married to the woman.

Delgatty grew hoarse and coughed his voice clear.

The priest smiled and sipped at his drink. He changed the subject.

And now you're off to Dublin to buy a greyhound. It's a fine life you're living for a man. A fine life. And you should remember to thank God for it.

It was Delgatty's turn to smile.

I do thank God. I think I'm OK with God, Father Ryan. We have a sort of understanding. I'm a rough Christian I am Father. He gives me a bit of rope.

Well make sure you don't hang yourself with it.

Delgatty silently forgave the priest for the predictability of his response.

But The Church and I have a distance between us Father Ryan.

I'm not talking about The Church Delgatty. I'm talking about God. The Church as a whole, I should say, has been trying to undermine God for centuries.

Delgatty was always impressed at the priest's candour.

And how's that Father?

Well the message is clear enough. All men, women and children are blessed with the grace of God and to simply and sincerely ask for forgiveness is for it to be granted. And to mend your ways of course. Every day is a new beginning.

That mending your ways is a real hurdle Father Ryan.

But every day you start afresh. How can that be a hurdle? You ought to go to church though Delgatty.

I'm all right on my own Father.

Ah but you're not. You lack edification.

I went to university Father Ryan.

Delgatty grinned at his own joke.

Very funny. We Christians need building up. We need the support of our church. It's so easy to lapse. Go to church, son. There's a big difference between The Church and church with a small c. You can go to church for edification and still criticise all you like Delgatty.

Yes I get you but answer me this though. When I went to secondary school, we had an assembly every morning. From the age of eleven to seventeen we sang every single day God be in my head and in my understanding.

Delgatty had won a scholarship to one of the old Grammar Schools in Birmingham.

You know the one?

Of course I do Delgatty. Henry Walford-Davies it was who wrote it. Your British government knighted him you know. Beautiful meditation of a hymn. And you sang it every day as a child?

Every school day for seven or eight years Father. You know the last line, God be at mine end and at my departing? *That always choked me up even when I was in the First XV. What I want to ask you is what would a man have to do for God to make the prayer he prayed daily as a child null and void?*

Father Ryan looked with stern amusement at Delgatty over his spectacles.

Null and void you say. What like a steward's enquiry and thrown out of first place like a dodgy greyhound.

Could he bless the child and condemn the man or what?

God can do what he likes Delgatty but for my money you and the child are inseparable. You'll be all right so yer will. I'd bet short odds on that result.

The priest had the bit of this hobby horse tightly between his teeth.

Take that Jews and Gentiles thing. Jesus was adamant that he came for the benefit of both. For those who meticulously followed the law and for those who didn't. But The Church thought that was far too liberal and started to introduce some small print; get-out clauses yer know. There are a few local exceptions.

The *local exceptions* obviously was a reference to the Father's own liberal parish in County Cork.

They like the idea of the few yer know. A narrow entrance to Heaven. Eye of a needle. If that's the size of it we might all as well pack it in now then.

To be honest Father I always thought Jesus was a something of a hindrance himself. He always seems tetchy to me. Bit of a miserable bloke for the son of God.

You'd be tetchy if you had hundreds of people following you everywhere when you were totally knackered. Like Elvis or The Beatles.

Delgatty sank his brandy and stubbed out his cigar in the tin ashtray. He spoke though the smoke.

You see Father Ryan my Philosophy course at college, brief though it was, taught me to be sceptical of so much. Faith I understand has to be just that. A jump in the dark but I need at least a little evidence. I know you'll say evidence nullifies faith but it just seems to me the gap is too big.

The gap between faith and evidence you mean Delgatty?

Just that.

Father Ryan took a pack of cards from his pocket, shuffled them and dealt Delgatty five of them. Delgatty turned them over. They were a random collection, a couple of twos, a queen, a ten and a jack. Only two cards held the same suit.

Decent hand or what?

Delgatty turned them face-up.

I'd probably bet on the twos.

The Father took the cards, put them back in the pack and shuffled them again. He dealt another five cards.

Delgatty picked them up. He had three aces and two kings.

How'd you do that Father? Full house.

Me? Sure I didn't do anything. It's all down to chance.

He dealt again. This time Delgatty picked up a club flush.

Come on Father. I'm not playing cards with you again.

You think these cards aren't random?

As he spoke he dealt five cards face up; ace, two, three, four, five of clubs.

Random? Of course not. You're fixing these cards Father.

When you saw the men landing on the moon and the photograph of the blue and green world suspended in dark mid-space illuminated by the sun, did you think that was random? And molecules and atoms and literature, art and philosophy? Random? Evidence you say. Da Vinci, Picasso? Evidence.

Yes Father. And cancer and grief and foxes and chickens.

Sure I know about the failure. The Garden of Eden got fucked up by the weeds for sure. We can't deny it. We still suffer. No point in saying everything in the garden is lovely.

Ryan dealt one last hand face up. All five cards were the nine of clubs.

Evidence.

That's some pack of cards you've got there Father.

The priest rose from his seat, laughed and slapped Delgatty on the back.

I got 'em for the Sunday school. They love 'em. Let's go back. We're nearly there.

They returned to the carriage as the train was entering Holyhead. The others were on their feet and preparing to get off. Diana stood arranging the collar of her white blouse and brushing the creases out of her blue, suede skirt.

Delgatty remembered where he had seen her before. She looked up and smiled directly at Delgatty as if she knew him too. She was the girl from his bullfight dream.

The small group walked up the ramps and through the pedestrian boarding tunnels. On board they joined the queue for sleeping berths. Delgatty opted for A1 which was a double cabin nearest the exit. He couldn't bear the idea of dormitory accommodation and anyway he was cash-rich at the moment.

He said goodnight to the others and went off to find his cabin. He threw his zip bag on one of the single beds and went down to the bar. The first class lounge was empty except for the barman who spoke with the singsong accent of North Wales with its exaggerated s's.

Lookss like it'ss going to be a rough crosssing, Ssir. Terrible coming ohfer it wass.

Delgatty finished his brandy and lit a cigar.

Another please.

He was alone and felt comfortable in the fact. The tannoy croaked.

Will all perssonss not trafelling pleasse leaf the vesssel. We are ssailing in fife minutess.

The engines increased their hum and Delgatty took his drink on deck to watch the ship leave harbour. Seagulls batted by in the blackness and pins of light flicked across the harbour walls. In the early middle of his life, his hands on the flaking rail, he looked at the mass of dark water ahead. He raised his glass.

Lord have mercy on you Mr. Cadman. Christ have mercy on us.

He dropped the cigar stump over the side and returned to his cabin. He pulled the cord on the light over the bunk. The air simultaneously blew cold from the metal grille over his head. He stripped to his shirt and pants and sat on top of the blankets looking through the current issue of *The Greyhound Owner* which carries the sales results of both British and Irish auctions.

The last time Delgatty had bought a dog in Dublin things had turned out badly. He'd paid four hundred and fifty guineas for a big, nervous, white dog weighing eighty odd pounds and the animal had broken a hock on only his second trial at Perry Barr. Pent House he was called.

Delgatty was advised by the vet to have him put down but he had persuaded him to strap the leg up so he could take the dog home and keep him in the vicarage garden shed. Pent House eventually had returned to soundness. He was never going to fulfil his original potential but he managed to win a couple of small races at Perry Barr and Delgatty, having done his duty of care by the animal, sold him to some bloke who wanted to flap the dog in East Anglia. They agreed on two hundred quid and the guy paid half of it up front but never paid the rest.

It was as the barman had predicted a rough crossing. He gripped the steadying rail against the diving of the boat; his face contorted in the mirror over the small sink as he sang.

Bye, bye Miss American Pie. Drove my Chevy to the levee but the levee was dry. Them good old boys drinking whisky and rye. This'll be the day that I die.

He snarled his mouth open and looked at his teeth in the mirror; his blue eyes were streaked with thin rivulets of red from the brandy. His hair, which totally covered his ears because of the fashion, was bleached blonder than normal from the March sunshine. He staggered against the cabin wall stabbing the inside of his cheek with the toothbrush.

For crying out loud keep still.

He stripped off and climbed into the bunk. Naked under the rough sheets he pulled the cord, leaving only the thin blue glow of the security light.

There was a knock on his unlocked cabin door. Somebody entered the cabin and closed the door.

It's me. Diana.

Diana?

Yes. There's something I want to know.

She sat on the edge of the bunk kicking off her shoes.

What are you doing Diana? What is it you want to know?

I'm the one asking the questions aren't I? Well the question anyway.

Well?

When you were playing cards someone said there were black twos a-floating. What does black twos a-floating mean? I like the sound of it.

Delgatty laughed.

A-floating? You mean like four calling birds, three French hens.

He laughed again and Diana joined in with him. The more they thought about it the funnier *black twos a-floating* became. Delgatty pulled the sheet round his naked body and the two of them began to stagger around the cabin laughing. Their joint laughter was incremental and they began to clutch at their aching stomachs.

Why didn't you ask Tom?

Delgatty managed to get the words out.

Tom is busy throwing up all over The Irish Sea.

And that just made them laugh even more.

Seven swans a-swimming.

Diana shouted randomly and Delgatty collapsed in pain on the bunk. She laughed and, moving with the sea, began to undo the buckle on her blue, suede skirt. The laughter gradually subsided apart from sporadic bursts from the pair of them.

Won't he be looking for you?

Shh. Anybody would think I wasn't welcome.

She placed a finger to her mouth in the blue dark. She folded her clothes neatly on the other bunk and was soon on her knees on Delgatty's bed pulling back the bedclothes.

He ran his hand down her naked back.

Move over then.

Delgatty got the picture.

17.

Esther Marie, kneeling on the carpet in front of the newly-lit coal fire, was delving into a cardboard box she had found in the old shed at the bottom of the garden. Delgatty had shoved a whole pile of boxes in there when he first moved in meaning to sort them out but he'd never found the time or the inclination.

Harriet had called in to check on her sister in Delgatty's absence.

O look Harri, our old hymn books.

I bet that's yours covered in brown paper, Esther.

Yes of course. I covered everything didn't I? Even now I get the kids at school to cover their books. It makes them last longer. It's their first homework for me.

Harriet took one of the books. On the front of her own hymn book Esther Marie's neat hand declared, *This is the property of Esther Marie Delgatty.*

Esther Marie opened the next, rather dilapidated one and on the title page her brother had written more peremptorily, *Delgatty Him's.*

He thought it was funny and it probably is.

Harriet's own hymn book read simply, *Martha Harry Delgatty.*

She showed her sister.

Didn't you spell Harri with an i in those days?

Apparently not. Look at these. Blimey they're Rupert Bear books. They were yours Esther and they're all covered in brown paper too. Maybe you've always been a bit of a weirdo.

Of course I have Martha.

Nobody's called me Martha since Mum and Dad died, bless them.

They smiled at each other and lowered their heads in a gesture of prayer.

Let's have some coffee.

18.

Delgatty arrived at the dog track at nine in a taxi. Men stood outside the stadium in bunches. They barked at each other. Delgatty had noticed this often. On an occasion when it is supposed to be exciting or just plain fun, like a day at the sales or a day at the races, men would stand in groups and laugh or it sounded like laughter but they were really only barking. Women did it too. He wondered what a research team of chimpanzees would make of it: all that facial grimacing and frantic noise.

He left his bag in the safe-keeping of the office, bought a catalogue and went upstairs to the restaurant. The others were already eating breakfast except for the priest who had gone on to his parish in Cork.

Morning Delgatty.

The cockney Skinner spoke through a mouthful of sausage.

They let you sleep on did they? They threw us off the boat at six. The joys of first class travel. They let you sleep in.

Diana raised the corners of her mouth in a smile at the appearance of Delgatty but didn't speak. The white-faced Tom was busy reading his catalogue. Delgatty joined them, immediately uncomfortable at the noise Skinner was making with his food.

There's some good dogs here Delgatty. If they all turn up.

Dogs entered for a sale sometimes are withdrawn either through lameness or the owner's change of heart.

Are you staying for tomorrow?

No I'm going back tonight.

We might stay Tom eh? We might stay eh?

Tom nodded behind the pink catalogue.

We might stay.

Delgatty turned to call a waitress, catching Diana's glance for a second. Her eyes were laughing. She spoke up with a fresh boldness.

Did you get a good night Mr. Delgatty?

Excellent thanks Diana. And you?

Well Tom wasn't too good so I had to find a corner on my own.

I had a lousy night. I had to leave Diana to her own devices. Sick as a dog.

Through the restaurant windows they could see a few owners walking their dogs in the middle of the track. A groundsman was tramping up the first straight with a rake. Staff were clearing the tickets that littered the betting ring; losers from the previous night's racing.

See that big fawn dog with the white feet? Down there by the paddock?

They all followed Skinner's finger.

That's Cobh Dancer. Fair dog that is. Done a good time round Limerick.

What would they be looking for for that?

Tom thumbed his catalogue.

You don't want that. I saw it on the way in. Feet like a frog.

Delgatty wasn't usually so negative but facts were facts. He remembered to eat for once and turned to the waitress without looking at the menu.

Full Irish please.

Feet like a frog? What's that supposed to mean?

Skinner drained his coffee cup, trying to save some face in front of his new sponsor.

It's how they run that counts, not what they bleeding look like.

Tell that to Judge, Skinner.

Tom was already putting a line through the dog in his catalogue.

He pushed back his chair and got up.

Come on let's go and have a look at a few of them.

Skinner stood up. Diana stayed put.

I'll be down in a bit Tommy. I'm a bit fagged-out.

A term Delgatty hadn't heard in years.

Diana had left in the night. She had shared Delgatty's cigar as she dressed. They were silent as the men left the restaurant and then they smiled.

I was wondering if you'd had eggs for your breakfast, Mr. D.

Why so?

Well on my way to the restaurant I saw six geese a-laying.

She said it so matter-of-factly she caught him unawares and they were off laughing again; the table and the dirty plates between them.

They pulled themselves together. Diana got up.

I'd better go and find Tom.

Delgatty got to his feet as she left the table.

Nice to see manners.

She made to leave the restaurant.

What does it mean? Black twos.....

Delgatty held up his hand.

Don't say it again for pity's sake. I'll be laughing all day. It means a black two, two of spades or two of clubs, can represent any card. So if you got two tens and a two of clubs you can claim to have three tens. There that's all it means.

Oh I see. That's not very funny is it?

Just tell me how a lovely woman like you hooked up with Tom. Bit of a mismatch, surely.

We're not hooked up. I just fancied seeing Dublin.

She kissed him on the lips.

I hope we meet again.

She turned and he watched her manoeuvre though the tables and out of the door.

After a contemplative pause he returned to studying his catalogue.

19.

The Delgatty family always had dinner at the table around seven o'clock or later on a Sunday when Luke had evensong in one or other of the churches in his Wolverhampton parish. Phyllis and Luke and the kids might well be accompanied for dinner by some vagrant or luckless soul who was staying at the time.

They said grace. They ate their meal and afterwards their mother and father would ask their guests and their own youngsters about their day and often too about their futures and expectations.

When the kids were teenagers their ambitions became a little more focused.

Harriet wanted to complete her education, marry, have three children and build a career in some sort of social services role. Oh and she wanted lots of shoes.

Esther Marie wanted to teach and build a home, hopefully with a loving husband but she was not so sure about having children.

School will be enough. I don't really need any more kids.

Delgatty came at the question more obliquely.

I want to live up a lane with a fire in a bucket.

Oh yes Philip Larkin. Toads *as I remember.*

Well remembered Dad.

Luke knew the poem by heart.

Their unspeakable wives are skinny as whippets and yet no-one actually starves.

What about university Jay?

Oh yes Mum I'll go to university all right like the girls. The only difference is I'll always have one eye on the fire in the bucket.

Speaking of whippets and starvation, isn't it time you fed your dog?

All in hand Dad. Just waiting for the carrots.

Delgatty at the age of fourteen had been given a dog, a greyhound. It was a bitch who had run at Monmore Green as Ruby Tuesday. She was a tiny thing, barely bigger than a whippet, and prone to wrist problems. Her owner was a wealthy patron at the Wolverhampton track and had bought her as a puppy. He had now given up on the bitch. One night he was approached by a fan of the singer Melanie who said he would like to buy her because of her name.

You can have her friend. Just take care of her and don't try to race her for a good while. She's lame.

Of course.

That same Melanie fan kept the dog as a pet. A few months later misfortune befell him and he became destitute, eventually finding himself a temporary lodger at the Wolverhampton vicarage. When he left he asked Phyllis if the family would take the greyhound. Delgatty had grown fond of the bitch.

O yes please Mum. Let's have her.

Delgatty did take good care of Ruby. Luke and he converted a shed as a kennel in the vicarage garden and built a little run in front of it to give the bitch space to empty. She was utterly stubborn and refused to piss whilst on the lead, however long the walk.

Gradually Delgatty noticed Ruby was walking more soundly and, late one evening, decided to let her off the lead in West Park, only ten minutes from the town centre. She galloped for joy and seemingly painlessly.

20.

Can I do any business for you Mr. Delgatty?

It was Michael. He was the perfect Irish gentleman and Delgatty had met him at the Dublin track before. He wore broken down, plastic shoes and looked like he probably slept rough. Delgatty liked to think Michael was an angel; an angel down on his luck.

Do you know the connections of Hurricane, Michael?

Sure I do Mr. Delgatty. It's my job to know.

Well you could ask them what they want for him, Michael please. I would be grateful.

The idea of Michael taking his *job* so seriously was touching to Delgatty. If he wasn't an angel, he was at the very least Mr. Bojangles in his worn-out shoes.

Michael soon returned, mincing his words.

If a puppy does anything at all at this time of year, yer know Mr. Delgatty.

How much?

Grimacing apologetically, Michael spat it out.

Two grand.

OK. I might as well have a look at his card Michael. He's fifty two. Would you also bring me eighteen, seventy six and ninety four.

When Michael returned from the office with the Irish Coursing Club documents he had requested, Delgatty checked out Hurricane's card. The pup had won four of his six racing starts at Clonmel and both his pre-racing trials. The other one had been a solo trial to get him started. Before Delgatty even set eyes on Hurricane he wanted him.

Skinner saw him looking at the documents.

Do you want me to find the owners and have a word with them Delgatty. See what sort of money they want, like?

Skinner vigorously scratched the back of his hand as he spoke.

Michael's already approached them for me Skinner.

Michael? What that scruffy bloke? Wouldn't do any harm for me to have a word with 'em. I've spoken to a couple of blokes for that Tom already.

Skinner thanks but Michael has already spoken to them. I don't want to look too keen.

Michael reappeared.

Mr. Delgatty I'm awful hungry.

Delgatty pulled a blue note from his pocket.

Get yourself some breakfast Michael.

And would you be having anything yourself?

Delgatty admired the generosity of the poor.

No thanks Michael. I've eaten.

Skinner took the opportunity to vent his annoyance with Tom.

He's a bloody idiot, Delgatty. He's after that brindle dog. Lot ninety four.

Oh really I was looking at that dog's card myself. What's wrong with it Skinner?

He's not raced Delgatty. Three qualifying trials and never raced. Wouldn't that make you suspicious? Never been seen by the public. Only run behind closed doors?

Skinner had a point; a good point.

If you'd qualified a dog to race wouldn't you want to…

Yes I get you Skinner. We'll have to watch him closely in his trial. He's not behind closed doors today.

Michael returned with a bacon sandwich and Delgatty kindly waved away the proffered change.

Just point out the owner of Hurricane, Michael please. Thanks for your help.

He indicated the direction of the owner with a nod of his head. Delgatty handed him another Irish fiver. As Michael retired to eat his sandwich Skinner eyed him begrudgingly.

Nice day's work for doing nothing.

Delgatty did not respond but approached Hurricane's owners, a well-dressed man and woman who were drinking Guinness and eating ham sandwiches for breakfast at the bar.

My name's Delgatty. I'm interested in your dog.

He smiled his introduction politely to them both but then addressed the man.

Will you take fifteen hundred?

The stranger put his half-eaten sandwich back on the plate and wiped his mouth. He spoke with an educated Irish accent.

Mister... Delgatty is it? We brought the dog to put him on the bench and that's what we are going to do. The reserve is eighteen hundred guineas and there's a lot of interest. If you want him we would be pleased if you would bid for him.

He returned to his sandwich. No deal. Angel or not, Michael had clearly pissed him off with his toings and froings.

Well thanks for being so straight about it.

He turned back.

I know it's a stupid question and I might not get him anyway but what's his kennel name. I'm superstitious about that sort of thing.

Higgins.

O brilliant. As in Alex the snooker player?

Yeah or maybe the bullfighter. His sire is Minotaur and his dam Pot Black so judge for yourself. We're really not sure. He's well named anyway. We bought him as a sapling, an investment yer know. We didn't breed him or name him.

Delgatty nodded his appreciation of the response and returned to his table. Hurricane was looking expensive, nearly as much as Delgatty had paid for his house four years earlier.

The loud speakers in the bar boomed into life with a recorded, trumpet fanfare.

Trials will start in 5 minutes Ladies and Gentlemen. I refer you to your catalogue. The runners in the first trial are Trap 1, catalogue number 36, Trap 2, number 33, Trap 3, number 37, Trap 4 is vacant, Trap 5, 41 and Trap 6, 42.

The times were slow. Only one dog broke 31.00 in the first five trials over five hundred and twenty five yards.

Delgatty went outside for Hurricane's trial. He wanted to get a good look at him and he wasn't disappointed. He was the most perfect greyhound he had ever seen. He wasn't flashy. He was straightforwardly handsome and athletic.

In Dublin the dogs are loaded into the traps at the side of the track and then swung out on to the racing circuit like in some canine fairground ride. It works well though and saves the starter and his loading staff churning up the surface of the course.

The hare whirred into action and tripped the lids of the traps. Hurricane, in Trap 5, missed his break by a couple of lengths but showed plenty of speed up the long straight to lead fractionally at the first bend. He pulled a length clear down the back but had done most of his running by the three quarters and only just held on by a short head at the line. The second dog was a year older and the time of 30.23 was impressive with the ground running at least a third of a second slow.

Delgatty went down to the kennels to check the dog out after the race. Hurricane, close-up, confirmed himself to be perfectly proportioned and Delgatty felt almost humble in his presence.

He had noted three possibilities in other trials and checked them out too, opening their mouths and looking at their teeth; a good indicator of their general health. Maybe he'd be able to buy more than one dog. Hurricane had to be the priority but if he didn't get him he couldn't return home empty-handed and waste all the expenses.

The sales will start at two o'clock sharp.

21.

Dad I think Ruby is sound now. I'd like to give her a run on a track.

You're fourteen Jay. Fourteen.

Yes but I think she'd enjoy it. I don't want a bet or anything.

And where would you want to run her?

A flapping track it would have to be. I don't have any papers for her.

And so it was that the family and the little bitch crammed into the Austin A40 and headed for Coalville one Saturday morning for the trials.

Delgatty eased her into the trap and watched little Ruby easily qualify to race over the sprint trip. You only need one trial at a flapping track.

She can run Tuesday night if you want son.

The racing manager marked her up.

Delgatty looked at his mum and dad. They nodded in unison.

If she's sound in the morning.

22.

In the bar Delgatty got a brandy and took it to a chair in the corner. He checked through his catalogue notes.

After the break he went back outside to the auction ring. The greyhounds were lifted one by one on to the sales bench roped off in front of the auctioneer's Punch and Judy box. The dealers and buyers stood or sat in the vicinity, leaning into the ring occasionally to examine the lots. Delgatty sat on the scaffolding benches directly in front of the auctioneer.

Lot forty eight, gentlemen is, a brindle, white dog.

Delgatty looked at his notes.

Fast up, clear ½ way. Not stay. Btn 2L 31.30

The auctioneer peered over his glasses.

Only a puppy and he showed a lot of pace today on this testing ground. He's won in 31 dead at Limerick last month. Start me at three hundred won't you? Come on now. Start me then. Right Sir, two hundred then. I'll take that for starters.

He turned to the owner behind his shoulder for his agreement.

Right he's on the market. At two hundred, two hundred guineas then standing to my right. I'll take a twenty. Thank you Sir. Two twenty seated dead opposite.

Delgatty dropped out at three hundred guineas and the dog was knocked down for three fifty. That reduced his options but there was really only one dog he wanted.

The next dog up was three years old and had finished tailed off in his trial.

Fifty for him then. I'll take fifty guineas. He got a bump at the first bend today so don't judge him on that.

After a long pause the auctioneer continued,

OK give me ten guineas for him. You know we can't go below that or he'll end up being experimented on somewhere.

Delgatty was half tempted to bid for the animal but was saved by a bid from the front. The dog was eventually knocked down for fifteen guineas so all was well. Greyhounds are expensive to keep so somebody obviously intended looking after him.

When Hurricane was put up Delgatty moved right inside the ropes. He ran his hands from the animal's shoulders right down to his quarters and looked hard at his feet. They were bunched tightly.

Perfect.

A lot of improvement in him. He'll be two in a couple of months I know but he's very much a puppy yet. A fine looking animal I'm sure you all agree, all seventy six pounds of him. Lot fifty two.

The eulogy was ending.

Delgatty climbed back out of the ring and stood to one side. At thirteen hundred he caught the auctioneer's eye by waving his catalogue sharply once.

New bidder at thirteen but you're going to have to do a bit better gentlemen. Fourteen is there?

Delgatty snapped his catalogue again.

Fourteen I have now. It's not enough but fourteen I have.

The man Delgatty had spoken to in the bar was still slowly shaking his head behind the auctioneer. The auctioneer pushed his glasses further on to his nose and spoke sternly to the small crowd.

Look we want to sell him but we can't give this lovely dog away. Come on now. Sixteen is there or I'll be taking him down?

Sixteen there was from somewhere at the back of the scaffolding. Delgatty started to turn away.

Come on now. I'll take a fifty.

Delgatty waved his programme again.

One thousand, six hundred and fifty guineas then I have. Gentleman standing to my right in the navy blue suit.

The owner gave a brief nod and turned to descend the ladder at the back of the loft. The hammer came down and that was that.

Delgatty completed the paper business, handed over the cash and shut himself in the phone box.

Marie I've been and bought a cracker. He's fantastic. He's the nearest thing to a mythical beast you will ever see.

What's his name?

Hurricane is his racing name.

*Wonderful! What do **we** call him?*

Higgins. I'm getting the ferry in a couple of hours and bringing him straight home. You'll love him.

Higgins. Oh he sounds like a butler.

Delgatty laughed to himself. Trust Esther Marie not to consider the snooker player or the bullfighter. When he hung up Skinner was waiting for him.

You got yourself a fair tool there Delgatty.

Nice young dog I do believe.

Will you be flappin' him?

I haven't been flapping for a good while Skinner. I'll take a pup to the flapping tracks for a handslip but since the permit licence I have stuck to NGRC.

The NGRC had finally recognised that people wanted to train their own dogs and not give them up to a registered trainer. They came up with an admirable system where individuals could register for a Permit Licence to train up to four greyhounds in their ownership.

You're right Delgatty. I packed the flappin' in when Brownhills opened. It's a better class of racing and a stronger market.

Skinner scratched at his bare arms as he spoke.

Delgatty didn't need to explain his position to Skinner but he was a political animal and wanted to. A man with his own greyhound only had one option until the early 1970's and that was to put the dog in the charge of a registered NGRC trainer where you were at the mercy of their whims. It was your dog but they looked after it and more or less decided when it had a winning chance. They might not even tell you.

So if you wanted to be in charge of your own and your dog's fate you would train it yourself and go on the flapping circuit. Delgatty had run Rex as far afield as Chester and Wisbech under names meant to deter possible backers like Free Gift or Last Chance.

That bloke whatisname?

Tom?

Yeah Tom. He bought that dodgy bastard, must be fucking mad. Gave three hundred for it.

Well I hope it turns out all right for them.

Him you mean. That Diane's gone.

Diana?

Oh Diana is it? Yes she's gone. Told Tom she wanted to have a look round Dublin and then fly home. He gave her the cash and she got a cab. Just like that. We'll probably never see her again Delgatty.

Normally Delgatty would have preferred this outcome but he found he did hope he would see Diana again and her enigmatic departure intrigued him.

It was half past twelve as the boat glided into Holyhead. He went down to the kennels in the bow of the boat, next to the mortuary. The dogs whined at his appearance. Higgins was in a large cage at deck level. Delgatty unbolted the door and caught the dog on the collar and lead. Higgins walked on to the deck and shook himself, glad to be out.

Good lad. That's better.

Higgins, not a nervous animal, moved his tail approvingly.

After the boat docked there was some nausea in the customs. The excise man, affecting some knowledge of greyhound racing, queried the receipt from the auctioneers. He studied the dog's Irish Coursing Club registration card.

Hurricane is it then? Nicely bred. 30 dead round Clonmel. He was cheap at six hundred and fifty guineas. Cheap at that.

Maybe you should've been there and bid for him yourself. I nearly left him there at that price I can tell you.

Delgatty paid the VAT in cash. Money for nothing. The law. The Irishman writing the invoice at the track, had made a slight adjustment to the actual price however to ease the pain a little.

You don't want to be paying all that VAT. A clerical error maybe. Six hundred and fifty of your lovely Irish guineas. There you are.

The train was already in the station at Holyhead and Delgatty went through to the platform. He muzzled the dog lightly to conform to yet more regulations and chained him to the rail in the guard's van. Although Delgatty was to remain with the dog throughout the journey he would inevitably fall asleep, his head on his travel bag, and the dog would be unsupervised. A chain was much safer than a lead. Dogs have been known to hang themselves when tethered by a lead.

Delgatty slept for an hour or so and the dog lay next to him with his head on his knee. Higgins had decided to trust this man.

The guard popped his head out of his cubby hole.

Sheffield next stop.

Delgatty lifted Hurricane down from the train, his bag slung over one shoulder, and carried him up the steps to the bridge and down the other side. He passed through the exit to the taxi rank. Dexter would be at work at this time of day so he'd have to take a cab. The first taxi on the rank declined to take them.

No Pal. No dogs in my cab. The boss' ruling, not mine.

I'll bloody well take you Sir.

He accepted the cabbie's offer. Inside the taxi the dog sat next to Delgatty on the bench seat and shook himself when his muzzle was removed, misting the rear window with his breath.

Bloody big isn't he?

Yes he's a big dog. Only a pup really but he weighs nearly eighty pounds.

I bet he eats a lot.

Delgatty instantly liked this amiable driver and enlightened him on the fundamentals of greyhound husbandry as they drove through the March sunshine. It didn't take long to emerge from the city and the driver had elected to drive through the villages of Killamarsh and Clowne rather than take the motorway.

I get sick of motorways. Same bloody price anyway.

Delgatty smiled.

Good of you to take the dog in your cab.

In my religion you are obliged to respect dogs. Even strays.

The driver grew earnest.

Dogs are very important to us. We believe they have spiritual vision. They guard the doors of heaven. I couldn't believe it when that cabbie refused to take you.

Is that Punjabi on the front of the cab there?

Delgatty was referring to the postcard pasted on to the dash board.

No no. We came over from India a few years ago but I'm Iranian not Indian. The Indians called us Parsis. Persians if you like. The postcard? It's a prayer. A kid's prayer really but we all say it.

We?

Yes me and my family are Zoroastrians. You probably say Zarethusa instead of Zoroaster.

O yes Thus spake Zarethusa *isn't it?*

No that's Zarathustra. Nietzsche. It was a philosophical treatise claiming God is dead.

Yes I know of it of course. I studied Nietzsche. Too many z's for me to take in. I've been travelling all night.

Ashem Vohu is the prayer on the postcard. It means, Blessed is he who is righteous for the sake of righteousness. *It's in Farsi but probably just bloody squiggles to you. We say it a lot but if I'm busy I just look at it a couple of times. It's better than nothing.*

What's your name?

Azad. It means free. Good for a taxi driver eh? Very low tariff.

You could be forgiven for thinking I was Indian. Parsis have lived there for centuries to escape persecution from Islam. We were there when the English ran the bloody place and they taught us to swear.

His eyes sparkled good-humouredly in the rear view mirror.

Bloody is OK Azad. It comes from the old English By Our Lady. *A reference to The Virgin Mary.*

Oh that doesn't sound OK to me. I better try and bloody well stop using it.

You seriously religious then Azad?

Course I am. This isn't a nightshirt and nightcap I'm wearing.

His eyes shone again in the mirror. Azad was dressed in a spotlessly-clean, tieless, white shirt, a white skull cap and had a white cord tied around his waist.

What's your name?

Delgatty.

Sounds Indian. Are you religious Delgatty?

No definitely not religious. I'm a Christian though.

And the dog?

No he's not religious. Well I don't think so anyway.

The driver laughed in the mirror.

I mean his name.

Dogs usually have two names. There's his kennel name which is Higgins. He knows that name.

Hello Higgins.

The greyhound swung his tail in response.

Yes he knows his name all right. Oh like that bullfighter?

Maybe, but I prefer the snooker player. So he's Higgins but his official racing name is Hurricane. He's registered as Hurricane. It's like me. My official name is Delgatty but at home they call me Jay.

Oh in the bloody dog house you mean.

Yes that's it. In the bloody dog house.

They drew up outside Delgatty's cottage.

Blimey is this your place?

Yes beautiful isn't it?

Must have cost a fortune.

Cost me two grand four years ago.

Worth treble that now with inflation.

Delgatty had bought it in 1970. He'd paid cash for it with his Nijinsky winnings. He would have won more only Piggott gave the horse too much to do in The Arc de Triomphe and finished second to Sassafras.

You're an estate agent too are you?

No but my cousin is. Where's this dog racing happen then? I might come.

Do you know Brownhills?

Sure I do. Got a cousin in Wolverhampton.

Is your family in Wolverhampton now?

No just my cousin and his wife. My family came over in the 1960's when I was about ten. We lived in bloody Hampstead for a while then a few of us started to move around the country a bit and I ended up in Derby, then Sheffield. I like it though. I'm a Yorkshire Persian now but I still have to go to London for our festivals.

The dog was getting a little restless but, before getting down from the cab, Delgatty wrote his phone number on the back of one of Azad's business cards.

Give me a call in a couple of weeks and I'll tell you when he is running. Or keep an eye on the dog racing in The Star. *They publish the Brownhills cards.*

I bloody well will Mr. Delgatty.

He paid the fare and climbed down, lifting the dog after him. Higgins pricked up his ears at the new surroundings, picking up his feet and putting them down without progress; beauty in the beast.

Azad watched them go before driving back to bloody Sheffield.

Delgatty took the dog around the side of the house which skirted the empty field next door.

We'll find you a rabbit in there lad.

The phone was ringing. He slipped the loop of Hurricane's lead over a paddock fence post and, finding the door locked, let himself in with the key they kept under a stone. Esther Marie was in the hall.

Jay. Sorry I forgot I locked the door. I was out in the kennels. I'll get the phone.

Hello. Oh Harri. Jay's home. You just missed him. He got a cab.

Harriet had been impatient to see Delgatty and the new dog and had driven to Sheffield to meet them.

Delgatty took the phone.

That was kind of you Harri. I'm sorry I missed you. The dog's tied up in the garden. I've got to go. Thanks again.

The pips rushed in and she was gone.

Come on. I can't wait another moment to see him.

Esther Marie ran outside to greet Higgins who gently moved his tail to show he approved of this new guardian in his life.

Oh he is wonderful Jay. Just look at him. What beautiful feet! And what a lot of ground he stands over.

I knew you'd like him.

As Delgatty kennelled the new dog, Rex became animated if not a little bolshie and Delgatty took the time to enter his kennel and fuss over him.

I'll put you back with Queenie tomorrow Rex boy.

He pulled the dog's ears lightly as a mark of affection.

Higgins can stay on his own. He won't bother you. Good boy.

I'm going to have a shower Marie. I'm knackered.

I'll stay here a while and get to know him a bit.

Delgatty returned to the house, took a brandy into the bathroom and turned on the shower. He sat in naked peace on the lavatory, the water drumming into the bath. He began to sing.

Goodbye Yellow Brick Road where the dogs are society hounds.

The simple things were what mattered after all.

You can't keep me in your penthouse I'm going back to my plough.

The simple things in life, a man washing and singing in the shower with a new star in the kennel and a couple of grand hanging in the wardrobe.

One day you are treading the grapes, the next you are drinking the wine.

Delgatty dried himself and pulled on the blue-towel dressing gown Esther Marie had given him for his twenty eighth birthday. In the bedroom he flipped though the record sleeves and put Terry Jacks' *Seasons in the Sun* on the stereo.

He finished the brandy and lay on the bed; speakers on either side of the room. The music crept into his dream.

We had joy, we had fun, we had seasons in the sun.

The stadium appeared vast, empty, ghostly before him. The runners moved slowly and silently with the music in his brain. Delgatty watched and shouted, making no sound.

It's hard to die when all the birds are singing in the sky.

Esther Marie came up the stairs and took the arm off the stereo; now clicking interminably on the wordless centre of the record. She shut the door on the sleeping man.

23.

Ruby had indeed been sound the next day, after her gallop in West Park, and the teenage Delgatty had read everything in the book his father had bought him about greyhounds, especially the chapter on preparing a dog to race. He didn't have a massage stool like it said in the book so he improvised with a couple of breeze blocks. He didn't have any liniment but he had found some menthol rubbing ointment in the bathroom cabinet. The little bitch must have thought she was on fire.

And on fire she was. She fled the traps like a bird in flight and arrived at the winning post yards in front of anything else.

The Delgattys cheered Ruby home and, of course, it was a Tuesday.

When Delgatty had washed the dog's feet and returned to meet his family at the car, his father handed him ten five-pound notes.

I couldn't let her run without a fiver on her. That'll keep her in meat and veg for a good few weeks. Well done Jay.

24.

Conrad just phoned me Dexter. Conrad you know the bloke at the funeral place. Yes him. I like him. He's coming with us apparently. He's bringing the ashes. Are you up for it tomorrow night? We're meeting in The Fleece *about eight. No the women aren't coming. Shall I pick you up Deck? If we drive to Sheffield we can leave the car there and get the train to Wolverhampton. OK see you then.*

Judge was already at the bar of *The Golden Fleece* with Father Ryan when Dexter and Delgatty got there. They'd nearly finished their first drinks when Conrad Joseph arrived, a plastic urn under his arm. Conrad had dispensed with the three piece, cream, disco-look suit he wore so incongruously in the funeral parlour. Tonight he was bedecked in checked, flared trousers, two inch platform shoes and a pink, silk shirt with a crimson, kipper tie. All this was topped off with his stunning Afro hairdo.

You look great Conrad. I hope you've got a coat somewhere. It's still only April. Is Yoko not coming?

No I've managed to shake her off for the evening. I don't need a coat. Spoil the look.

He didn't look directly at Delgatty but at himself in the mirror behind the optics.

Anyway I thought it was no women.

You can't say No women *these days, Conrad. This is the 1970's but yeah you're right. It's men only tonight.*

Punch and Tony arrived together on foot and the party was complete. Punch drank his cokes, Judge his orange juices and the others drank Brew X1 with whisky chasers. Conrad was the star of the evening. It was probably his first ever night with the boys and he quickly became inebriated.

Delgatty had found this fay man amusing from the time he had first met him only a couple of weeks before. What amused him now was that even in his drunken and garrulous state he remained immaculate and went to the lavatories in between each round to wash his hands and make persistent use of his Afro comb.

Yoko is a lovely girl. A beautiful girl even but she's not as beautiful as me is she now?

He looked, wide-eyed, to the group for agreement which was readily forthcoming in the form of general nodding.

Beautiful yes but not as beautiful as you.

Delgatty kissed the young man on the forehead.

Oi, Jimmy Hendrix, it's your round, Youth.

Dexter laughed at his own musical allusion to Conrad's ethnic roots. Conrad's father had migrated from The West Indies to Birmingham in the early 1940's and had flown with the RAF. Conrad had migrated from Birmingham to Wolverhampton in the 1960's.

Tony spent the early part of the evening attempting to pick Conrad's professional brains.

So what was the best funeral you attended? What would you say Conrad is the optimum length? I thought forty minutes.

Tony we have a thing called a Pre-Funeral Arrangement, that Dad and I are working on. It's an idea from America. You could be our first PFA customer. We'll talk about it some time.

Conrad clearly didn't want to talk shop just then and Tony realised that, although the place was fine, it wasn't really the right time and he desisted.

Even Punch grew talkative and in his way wanted, on this commemorative occasion, to put some flesh on the company's understanding of his friend Terry Cadman.

Well you all know he was Australian, don't you?

They hadn't known but it did explain the odd tint to the Black Country dialect that was Cadman's own.

He fought in France; fought like a fuckin' tiger. He stayed over here after the war and just well, stayed like, but he was never happy unless he was moving round the country. That's why the tipster lark suited him, see?

He was a wanderer, see? He never felt at home anywhere. He had this idea there was this woman he had to find. He didn't know who she was but he couldn't go back till he'd found her. Sounds daft don't it? True though.

He thought he found her and he did marry and they had kids.

He's got kids you say? We ought to get in touch with 'em.

He had two but one of 'em got killed. Some sort of hunting accident.

A hunting accident? What in Wolverhampton?

Dexter couldn't believe it.

No it was out Stafford way. He couldn't cope and left. Long time ago. He never found her. Her, if you know what I mean.

What about his other child?

Delgatty was concerned that he was depriving a next of kin of their inheritance.

Terry said she married for money and went to Australia. He lost touch with her years ago.

Punch was sensitive to Delgatty's point though.

Terry gave you that money Delgatty. Don't worry about it.

The bell rang for last orders and the small group of men toasted Cadman one last time, drank up and left the pub. Conrad scuttled back just in time to retrieve the forgotten urn before the doors were barred.

Cadman had been warned off all racecourses for five years or more and the group intended to redress this authoritarian injustice; not just for that night but for eternity.

One by one they climbed the fence surrounding Wolverhampton racecourse. Each put his foot into the hands of the following man for leverage until only Conrad was left on the wrong side. Punch hung over the fence and picked him up with one simple heave.

Watch the shirt Punch for crying out loud!

He had to put him down again however as Conrad had left the ashes on the ground.

Forgive us our trespasses.

Father Ryan laughed at his own joke.

Just look at the state of me.

Conrad actually looked no different.

They assembled at the five furlong start and flirted with the idea of dashing down the straight but the Father had clicked into ceremonial mode.

In the name of the Father and of the Son and of The Holy Ghost. Amen

Amen.

The word came raggedly from the group of men.

Father Ryan continued to intone as they walked slowly up the straight, the scene of News from Thebes' win, and they took it in turns to scatter a handful of Cadman to the clear night air and into the black turf.

Man born of woman has but a short time to live. Like a flower he blossoms and then withers. Lord have mercy on us.

Christ have mercy on us.

Delgatty's response was automatic.

And then the Father added rather more colloquially.

No man is happy until he is dead and buried.

Or scattered.

Conrad was trying to be helpful.

Cadman was distributed and the group, now solemn, aided each other back over the fence and that seemed to be that. Justice of a sort had been done or it had started to be done.

25.

Spring dawn in the sky, Delgatty came through the broken hedge into the wet lane enveloped in the steam of the mingled breath of man and dogs. Higgins was still full of scope but his first two ribs and pin bones were beginning to show as evidence of his fitness. Delgatty had been getting some strong roadwork into him before galloping him. Racehorses can be introduced to gentle work, breezing along under the restraint of a rider. Greyhounds have no such fetter and go flat out. They can easily damage a shoulder or a wrist. It is the trainer's art to produce them fit for galloping but with improvement to find.

Delgatty saw no harm in letting a dog have breakfast a couple of hours before a trial. That would just take the edge of his speed without causing any distress. He might even worm a dog out the day before a trial leaving the beast a little listless. Worm it out properly with a garlic solution which would go through a dog in twenty minutes and throw a pile of the horrid creatures like spaghetti on the ground. Try doing that with a packet of tablets from the pet store.

He broke a few slices of brown bread into an aluminium bowl and squeezed half a pint of milk, never water, to render the mixture sloppy. Higgins ate the lot in ten seconds flat.

Trial for you today son. Trial today.

Delgatty had never resorted to chemicals to slow a dog down. He had been in the game since his teenage years and knew that stopping dogs was a bad business. He'd seen it a hundred times at the flapping tracks; dogs nailed to the floor, running listlessly, collapsing with cramp even. The next time they'd want their dog to win. They'd break its heart and then expect it to win. And Delgatty, amongst others, took the view that this happened at the big tracks; well-known trainers with other people's dogs. It was however impossible to prove.

When Delgatty arrived at Brownhills Stadium the trials were already under way. The dog whined behind the grille in the back of the old Vauxhall estate. He could hear the mechanical hare.

All right. Steady son.

He went round to open the back, carefully catching Higgins with lead and collar attached. Unlike ordinary dogs greyhounds have collar and lead donned and removed together. They don't sit around in collars. He eased him on to the cinder car park.

An old gent with a clipboard was embroiled in an argument with two men. He indicated the blue brindle dog held by one of them.

I told you that dog can't run here no more without a trial. He got the red light. Take him somewhere else or you'll have to trial him in again here.

He's only won three fucking lengths.

The flat cap gesticulated his irritation.

Yes but he's found fifteen lengths since his last run. You know the rules you can find a second but no more. Take him off.

A second in time is equivalent to about twelve lengths in space.

Delgatty frowned. No art in those bastards. They take a delicate mechanism and hit it with a sledge hammer to slow it down a bit just to win a few quid.

The man with the clipboard turned to Delgatty.

Hello Sir. How are you and how is my favourite bitch Atalanta?

She's fine. In season at the moment but she'll be back soon.

Is this feller booked in?

Yes Sir. I phoned yesterday.

The old man consulted his board.

Ah yes. Black dog wide runner. Yes he's booked in all right. He's in the seventh trial. We're on the second now. Go in.

Delgatty kept the lead short as he walked in through the main gate. The owners of the previous runners were picking their dogs up at the brake; the hare now having gone to ground under a small wooden box. Brownhills Greyhound Stadium boasted an outside hare which was much better for trouble-free racing. An inside hare is usually only found at flapping tracks, as it is much cheaper to install, but does tend to create crowding at the bends.

He went straight to the paddock where he was approached by the racing manager.

It's a good few weeks since we saw you Sir.

He knew who Delgatty was of course but didn't use his name as track managers have to be discreet. Trial watchers never miss a trick.

Shall I mark him up now for you or do you want to trial him first? In case he doesn't grade?

He winked mischievously at Delgatty. They both knew, barring accidents, there was no chance of one of Delgatty's dogs failing to achieve a grading time. Delgatty went along with the wink.

What's the grading time for two six five yards?

A dog has to meet the grading time to qualify to run in a race.

18.50.

Mark him up now please.

Delgatty put his hand under Higgins's belly and stood him straight. The racing manager eyed the dog up and down and began writing on the card which would be Higgins's passport from now on and would allow him to race in Great Britain.

What do you call him? Hurricane?

He checked the name on The Irish Coursing Club document.

We'll stick with the Irish name, Hurricane. We flirted with changing his name to his pet name, Higgins. And before you ask, I prefer the snooker player to the bullfighter.

You can change a dog's name but it is regarded as bad luck.

Hurricane it is then.

The two white toes on Higgins's near hind were recorded, the single light toe nail on his offside fore, the flecks of white in his tail.

There are many stories in dog racing of ringers where men claimed to have two identical dogs, one unable to raise a gallop and the other catching pigeons but such tales are generally apochryphal. Some even claimed to have painted out the white toes on such and such a dog. You wouldn't get a ringer past this man, black paint or no black paint

Let's put him on the scales then.

Higgins's weight was recorded at thirty five kilos and he had to be within a kilo of that weight when next entered to run a race proper. A little more fluctuation was allowed for trials as a dog may be returning from lameness and be a short of condition or a bitch might be returning from season and be carrying too much condition. As Brownhills was an official NGRC track they were now recording weight in kilos and the distance of races in metres was in the offing.

I think I've got him now. Where does he run?

Wide. Especially first time round here I should think. Can you make sure he's not in with any headcases?

Don't worry he's in a four dog race with a dead railer and two rather slow individuals! Do you want me to book him in for his other two trials now or do you want to phone in?

NGRC tracks require three trials as evidence of a dog's ability.

No thanks I'll phone in. I'm superstitious about that sort of thing. I'd like to get him graded quickly though. By the end of next week anyway.

Greyhounds can take sprint races in quick succession, sometimes a dog might run twice on the same day, so three in ten days or so would not be too testing.

No problem we're here three mornings every week but Saturday is usually our busiest time.

Delgatty made his way to the side of the track as the dogs in the sixth trial flashed past making Higgins leap at the end of his tether. He pulled the racing muzzle on to the dog and coated him up in the black and white stripes of the six jacket. The other three dogs looked well cared for with the exception of a mangy blue dog in the orange five jacket. There were sores on its quarters from sleeping on bare boards.

What's a bale of straw cost for Pete's sake?

Take the runners for Trial Seven to the starting traps.

Higgins was still only a puppy but he knew his job. He calmed down at once and walked like a veteran to the boxes. Delgatty deftly held his underbelly with his right hand, whipping the collar and lead from the dog's neck with his left, and slid him gently into the back of the trap. The starter eased down the door at the rear of the trap.

Delgatty ran round to the front to make sure all was well. Just occasionally dogs, especially young dogs, manage to turn themselves round in the traps in their anxiety to begin the chase. Higgins was quiet and low and waiting.

Delgatty moved inside the track to watch, the lead hanging round his neck. The starter was happy all was well and waved his flag to the hare driver. The hare hit the switch and the traps flew open.

This was only a trial but Delgatty could never watch one of his dogs run without his stomach churning. He'd watched them land gambles, he'd watched them get beaten, he'd watched them for joy but he had also watched them break down.

He need not have worried this time. Higgins was three lengths in front after twenty yards. He checked wide at the first bend and lost yards but ran away from them down the back straight. He came to the hare brake on his own.

The voice from the speaker came hesitantly.

First number six. Then one, two and five.

Distances. Eight lengths, three quarters and twelve. Winning time 17.16

Delgatty had 17 dead on his own watch.

Perfect.

Good run that Delgatty. Fucking 'ell he pissed round there didn't he mate?

It was Skinner.

Yes Skinner I was quite pleased with that.

Skinner stooped down to scratch his shins through his trousers.

Bet you were. Fucking 'ell he pissed round didn't he though?

Delgatty had forgotten about Skinner but would have to think about him now if he was to pull off a gambling coup first time up with Higgins.

26.

When Delgatty got home Esther Marie, whose health was improving day by day, was not there and a note said she had gone to spend the day with sister Harri. They were going to see *Monty Python and The Holy Grail* for a bit of light relief on a quiet afternoon when the cinema would be practically empty. The picture house in Creswell had been called Rogers after the first owner but when it was sold the name had been changed most economically by switching a couple of the neon letters. These days it was called Regors.

Good on you Marie. There's a brave girl.

There was a message on the answerphone from Elizabeth, Dexter's Mum. Delgatty had never had a message from her before and phoned back straight away.

A distraught Elizabeth broke the news that Dexter had had a heart attack completely out of the blue and died. He'd just been pulling on a boot to play football with a few mates at the local council pitch when he collapsed. He was dead by the time the ambulance got there.

Jesus Elizabeth. God rest his soul. Is there anything I can do for you? I know everyone says that but if you need a lift anywhere or anything...

Delgatty had first met Dexter at the Waterloo Cup in 1969. They had started chatting at the meet before walking together to Withins Fields waiting for the frost to thaw and the stewards to announce coursing could begin. It was the first time either of them had been to the greyhound coursing blue riband.

A mate of mine's got a dog running. What about you, Youth?

Dexter called most men *Youth,* regardless of their age.

I've come with a bookie friend of mine. We just had a laugh. A bloke came up to him and said, What price the red collar in this first course? 1/2, *he said. The bloke had fifty quid.*

Dogs are identified in coursing by the collar they wear; a simple knitted red or white collar is slipped over their heads. The red collar always runs on the left of the two dogs.

Then another bloke asked, What price the white collar? 1/2, *he said again. And this guy had fifty as well.*

What did your mate do?

What would you have done? He shut the bag!

According to public mythology bookmakers are supposed to win all the time but it was actually rare to have a book where you couldn't help but win whatever the result.

They climbed to the top of the bank and stood together amongst the crowd. The frost had gradually disappeared and the judge entered the scene on his grey hack, his red hunting coat contrasting starkly with the green acreage of Withins Field; a more or less straight course where speed is the first requirement in a dog.

The other course at Altcar is on Lydiate. This is a huge rectangular field where the dogs cover more ground and need to demonstrate their coursing skills as well as their pace.

The slipper, also red-jacketed, seemed to appear from nowhere with two dogs collared-up and straining at the end of the dual leads or slips. He concealed himself behind the green hide, known as the shy, in the centre of the field. The crowd grew conspiratorially silent.

Somewhere deep in the country the beaters had done their job and a hare stood on the edge of the running ground considering its next move. It decided to cross. It appeared to realise the extreme danger of the great grassy expanse and sprinted past the shy intent on seeking the safety of the reeds and old rhododendrons at the far side of the field. The slipper seemed to give the hare a massive start before slipping the two dogs simultaneously, fully one hundred yards behind the fleeing creature.

The dogs quickly reduced the gap being far superior in speed over a distance of ground. The hare had a quicker burst of initial speed but could not sustain it. However the hare had its own advantage in the agility of its turns. The dogs with their relatively great size turned more slowly.

Good coursing greyhounds work together to the disadvatage of their quarry. A single dog would have little or no chance coursing a hare. Delgatty had seen hares run a dog ragged. He'd seen a dog lay down exhausted and the hare, in no hurry to quit the scene of its victory, sitting some twenty yards away apparently laughing at the hunter.

This hare was now back in the centre of the field and the jaws of the dogs snapped at every turn; snapped on thin air at each attempt. The judge awards points to each dog on the basis of their speed and their skill in turning the hare. In this instance the hare took the dogs to the very bottom of the bank at Withins Field, turned ludicrously sharply leaving the dogs out of their ground, and dashed through the crowd to safety. It passed within a yard of Delgatty and Dexter and they were full of admiration for the animal's courage and inventive exit. Had the hare, even under the duress of the chase, devised a plan and executed it perfectly or was it merely responding to instinct?

Greyhounds have no great amplified sense of smell and rely on their sight to chase their quarry. They are known as gaze hounds and the hare readily confused them by this tactic. It would normally steer well clear of humankind but this time it was its only chance of escape and much the lesser of the two evils confronting the animal.

The judge held up his red handkerchief and the dog with the red collar was through to the next round of the Waterloo Cup. The hare was through to the next day of its life and, with a bit of luck, might live another four years or so.

This had been a perfect start to the day; a good course where the skills of the dogs were demonstrated markedly and the hare had deservedly escaped. This was what everyone wanted to see and the crowd were exhilarated by this thirty second, gladiatorial spectacle.

You feel part of history don't you Dexter?

Dexter wasn't so sure.

Delgatty talked on of how the animals were first bred by Egyptians at the beginning of biblical times, how hares were introduced to

Britain by the Romans and how rules for coursing were first drawn up in Elizabethan times.

If you say so, Youth.

The Waterloo Cup is the premier coursing event in the world. For almost one hundred and forty years it has proved the ultimate test of a greyhound and each year sixty four dogs come from Great Britain, Ireland and as far away as America to participate in the knockout competition for prizemoney and silverware.

As with so many great sporting events, the special quality of the Waterloo Cup is the ground over which it is run on the Altcar estate near Southport. The Waterloo Cup wouldn't be the same anywhere else. You wouldn't want to play the FA Cup Final anywhere but Wembley after all, although they occasionally did of course.

The key factor about Altcar is the going. The peat beneath gives a springy texture to the surface of the turf and gives the dogs the confidence to let themselves down and stretch out fearlessly.

The next course was delayed by the appearance of a leveret on the running ground . The crowd laughed affectionately at the little creature and waited patiently for it to cross to safety before normal business could be resumed. Sometimes a rabbit strays on to the field and a similar wait is necessary. The crowd were there to see a contest not an execution.

The second course of the day introduced Dexter's friend's dog to the competition. He was called Hunter and was wearing the red collar. Hunter gained three points from his rival by leading up from the slips and showing the greater pace to turn the hare first. Dexter yelled him on.

The hare cut back into the centre of the field but was quickly brought down by his pursuers. One of the pickers-up was quickly on hand to remove the hare from the jaws of the two dogs and dispatch it with a blow to the back of the head. It is the job of pickers-up to prevent unnecessary suffering. Indeed anyone at a coursing meeting is duty-bound to dispatch the hare if it is brought down close to them.

The judge held his red handkerchief aloft and Dexter cheered the victor.

I've had twenty quid on him to win the whole thing at 20/1, Youth.

Well done. A long way to go though Dexter. Did you not back him to win this heat then?

No he was no price. 1/2. Must've bin thar mate.

The next few courses moved smoothly along and in each instance the hare escaped into open country. The hares, after all, are on their own territory and totally familiar with the terrain. There are no deterrents to their escape apart from their canine pursuers.

Delgatty took out a hip flask and offered his new friend the first swig. They talked about dogs and Delgatty said he was looking for a place with enough room to kennel half a dozen dogs but he didn't have the cash to buy so he would have to rent.

Leave it to me Youth. I'll find thee summat.

Dexter was true to his word and although Delgatty had not really considered Derbyshire it was as good as anywhere. Harriet and Esther Marie both lived there and property seemed cheap. Dexter found the place Delgatty now owned by talking to people in the village clubs. He was excited at the prospect of Delgatty and his dogs coming to one of the villages and shared his thoughts with his many cousins.

It'll be great to have a proper dog man int area. Someone who knows 'is stuff tha knows.

When's he comin'?

E'll be 'ere soon enough when ah've sorted him a place aht.

In fact Delgatty was able to buy outright the property Dexter had proposed thanks to Nijinsky's incredible series of wins in 1970. He had been at Newmarket when Lester Piggott won The Dewhurst on the two year old colt by an effortless four lengths and decided there and then to seriously invest in the animal's classic, three-year-old career.

Nice drop o' whisky that.

The two men stood together for the remaining courses of the morning. They exchanged phone numbers and enjoyed a black pudding together during the lunch time break.

I'm going to have to leave you Dexter. I've got dogs to do at home and it'll take me nearly three hours to get there.

Alreight Youth. I'll be in touch wi'thee.

Delgatty collected his bookmaker friend on his way to the car.

You had enough Bob? I'd like to get off.

Yeah that's enough for me. I've won a few quid but there's not a lot of money about.

I'm not surprised at your prices.

Delgatty checked the afternoon's results the next day and Hunter had unfortunately been eliminated in the next round so Dexter had lost his twenty quid.

Only a year later the men were firm friends; Dexter occasionally helping out with the dogs and the house renovations. He got on especially well with Delgatty's mother and father.

God and creation are not normally the sort of subjects that men easily discuss with each other. Dexter could barely write but he was one of the sharpest men Delgatty knew. They frequently opened up to each other.

Creation is flawed, Dexter. People go on about what a wonderful thing Nature is. Nature does us in. Nature will kill us all in the end. Look at that field.

Delgatty swept his arm across the flat panorama. The field had a crop of barley which was still young and green.

The way that hawthorn hedge is sculpted with such sharp angles. That's not Nature. That's art that is. The farmer did that, not Nature.

These dogs we love, they're half animal sure but then there's what we put into them. There's what they learn - skill, artistry. They talk about God and Nature as if they are the same thing. God is the opposite of Nature. He's an artist.

And He don't look back.

Dexter knew the Dylan lyrics. He laughed.

You and your fucking ideas.

The service was conducted in the red brick church in the village. Except for Esther Marie, who said she would stay home and prepare lunch, and Penelope, they were all there. Harriet sat between Delgatty and Mary, Tony, Conrad and Yoko sat just across the aisle a row in front of Judge and Punch.

Father Ryan had been invited by the vicar to preach the sermon; a most enlightened gesture in this protestant stronghold. He sat facing the congregation in the ornate chair reserved for visiting bishops. He was led to the pulpit by a frocked verger bearing a mace of some sort. They bowed to each other and Ryan, wearing a simple black cassock, mounted the steps and began.

In the name of the Father, Son and Holy Spirit. Amen.

John Dexter loved his family. He loved his Mum, Elizabeth and his Dad Zak, his sister Alice, his nephew Mark and his many relatives throughout the village. And they loved him. That's a great thing now, isn't it so?

And Dexter loved his football. Sheffield Wednesday meant a lot to him. When he couldn't get to a game he'd be first in the queue at the newsagents on a Saturday evening to pick up the local sporting paper which I believe you call The Green'un.

The congregation nodded.

Father Ryan picked up one of the books he had earlier placed on the pulpit shelf.

This book is called Football Association: The Laws of the Game. *The Laws of the Game now. And it would be nice to think that the laws never get broken. But they do. It would be impossible to play the game without breaking a few of the rules at some time. I'm not talking about cheating of course although that does go on - a crafty hand ball or pinching a few yards with a free kick - but inevitability the players will fail to comply with all of the rules all of the time.*

When a player is travelling at speed into a tackle there will be times when, through misjudgement, he hits the man instead of the ball and commits a foul. He will probably put his hand up to the referee to acknowledge his error and the game goes on. Sometimes the fouls are deliberate because players, through the will to win, give in to weakness and wrong-doing.

If the referee were to throw the rule book at everyone in breach of a rule in any particular game there would be no game. We'd have an empty pitch with all the players in the dressing room.

The priest took another book from the shelf and held it aloft.

This is The Bible.

He opened the book.

The Old Testament. The Laws of the Game if you like. Anybody ever broken any of the laws in here? Anyone ever been greedy or envious or spiteful? Of course. We all have. We all have. Even our dear departed Dexter will have.

Did you see The World Cup in Mexico on the television? They introduced a card system where the players get a yellow card shown to them by the referee for a first offence and a red card for a second or more serious breaking of the rules. A red card means you're off the field. No arguments. It's a good idea and I believe it's coming over here.

A long, long time ago it looked like everyone was breaking the rules and God got angry and for a while we did end up with an empty pitch. The story tells us there was just Noah, his wife and the animals and everyone else red-carded.

He flicked through the book to Matthew's gospel.

The New Testament now. The New Laws of the Game. The new agreement between God and us. The Laws are still there for us to try to follow but the difference is we have grace and forgiveness for failure, instead of punishment for failure. The Bible tells us it'll be Jesus who judges us.

So what's Jesus going to do about it eh? Is he going to red card the lot of us? Is he going to send us all to the dressing room? Maybe send the lot of us to Hell? Because we didn't keep the rules?

Hell no. Hell no.

We cannot earn our way into the presence of God. We can of course put our hand up and acknowledge our faults like the football player and the game can go on. Putting our hands up is, in effect, what we do when we pray. The game must go on. It is through grace that we are to find our way into heaven; not through our own efforts. It's through grace and forgiveness.

That doesn't mean we shouldn't try to keep the rules but we are bound to fail at times. We are bound to fail. We are imperfect. It's not the end of the world to err. We will be saved by what we believe. What we believe and not what we do.

I know Dexter believed. He told me. We trust he is in Heaven. And we trust that one day we will all, all, join him there.

As the priest was escorted from the pulpit by the verger, Tony took out his notebook and wrote something in it. Delgatty leaned forward and looked enquiringly across the aisle. Tony held up nine fingers.

After the service the procession moved, slowly on foot behind the hearse, to the small cemetery at the top of Creswell where the men were buried from the village pit disaster of 1950. The priest conducted the committal and family and friends passed in turn to the edge of the clay grave to throw a handful of soil on to the coffin that held Dexter's body.

Delgatty was seized by the desire to call out to his old friend but thought the assembly might misunderstand if he suddenly shouted, *Yoo faaackiing baaarstud* into the hole in the ground and so he adopted instead a prayerful posture simultaneously crossing himself and articulating into the grave a whispered staccato impression of Michael Caine.

Yoo. Facking. Barstud.

For several months after Dexter died Delgatty, when returning with the dogs in the early evening, would take a pull on the leads at his gate and listen. It was not difficult to imagine Dexter's voice on the wind and sometimes Delgatty was convinced he could hear it. He would yell at the stars.

Yoo fackiiinng baaarstud!

The dogs would wince but smile at their man when Delgatty gave them a reassuring look.

What comforted him most of all about it was the idea of Dexter, all done up in ballooning, white heavenly garb and sitting amongst the angels, suddenly letting rip in an earthwardly direction.

Yoooo faaaackiiing caaaant!

27.

Delgatty sat on the edge of the bed and blew his cigar smoke into a shaft of sunlight. He picked up the bedroom phone, holding the cigar between his lips and narrowing his eyes to keep the smoke out of them.

The phone rang in his lap, startling him for a moment.

Azad. Excellent. I hoped you'd ring.

Oh good you saw it in the paper. Yes he runs tonight at Brownhills. Keep it under your skull cap though. We don't want.....

OK I'll look forward to seeing you there. Meet us in the bar about seven thirty. He runs at eight o'clock. Are you allowed to drink? Good man Azad. See you tonight.

He held down the rest for a second and dialled Tony's number. Mary answered.

Jay my lovely. When am I going to see you? How's Marie? Has she forgiven Harriet and me for not helping with the lunch.

When the party had got back from Dexter's funeral, the usually patient Esther Marie had been slamming the plates around as she served the food and was obviously annoyed that she had been left to get the lunch on her own. When Harriet asked her what the matter was she complained that she would like to have gone to the service with Delgatty as well and that maybe just once Harriet and Mary could be a little less selfish.

Yes that's all forgotten. She just got into a bit of a state that's all.

Oh good. I wouldn't upset the lovely woman for the world.

Mary handed the phone to Tony.

Hi Jay.

Tony the new dog you saw in the kennels is ready to run and we're going to do a job at Brownhills. He's had his three qualifying trials and improved a couple of lengths each time. He's running in a race proper for the first time tonight.

Is this going to be the sort of job where we bet six hundred quid and say how unlucky we all were?

Now Tony when did that ever happen?

Well there was that dog at Perry Barr. Got knocked over at the first bend and ......

OK it happened once. Take your tablets you miserable swine. We'll see you tonight.

28.

The night Higgins won at Brownhills it was important that Delgatty paid his one hundred and fifty pound Perry Barr debt to Laverman before the race. He didn't want him thinking he was being paid with his own money.

And Higgins did win and they were all there. Judge, Tony, Dexter, Punch, Esther Marie, Harriet, Conrad, Yoko, Father Ryan, Azad and Delgatty. Penelope had cried off at the last minute.

Skinner was there too but Punch had said he wanted a word with him. Punch brought his old corner's boxing stool whenever Delgatty had a dog running and sat outside the racing kennel as the ultimate security device. The wooden racing kennels were simple and bare and circled the paddock like Victorian beach huts.

Yeah I want a word Skinner.

Skinner kept looking towards the betting ring dismayed at the lack of contact with his usual beneficiaries.

What they pay you Skinner when you tell 'em a dog's off?

They don't pay me anything. What you mean?

What they pay you Skinner?

Couple of nicker. Fiver sometimes.

You stay with me Skinner. You keep away from 'em till after Delgatty's dog has run and I'll give you twenty quid. OK?

Yeah OK.

But Skinner was not OK and still hankered to run to the ring and blurt the news for habit's sake.

Put your hands in your pockets Skinner and sit on this stool. You're going nowhere. You stay here and make sure nobody comes near that dog. I've got to put a couple of bets on.

It was as if Skinner was invisibly tethered to the boxing stool like a reluctant debutant waiting to enter the ring. The only ring he wanted to enter was, for once, forbidden to him.

Just give me fifteen quid Punch and put me a fiver on the dog.

OK.

Father Ryan kept his distance from the group. He was not well-known in England and most importantly he had not previously been to Brownhills which made him a principal player in the betting plan which was not to put a penny on the dog until one minute before the off. By that time the bookmakers would imagine the dog was unfancied.

Azad arrived looking rather lost in this strange environment where his white shirt and skull cap were the objects of many stares. Delgatty spotted him, bought him a coke and introduced him to the coterie, adding that this new friend was, rather exotically, a Zoroastrian.

Tony was especially keen to befriend Azad and it wasn't long before he introduced the topic of funerals.

So you really have a funeral pyre?

No that's the Sikhs. Well they used to anyway.

So what do you have Azad?

I'm happy to tell you Tony but how long is it to the bloody race? I think I'll have twenty quid on him anyway. Sounds good to me.

It's nearly an hour away. Nobody is to back it until the last minute. I'll show you what to do.

OK. What can I tell you?

Azad filled Tony in on the basics of the way Zoroastrians dealt with death. He went through the specifics of the funeral in detail Tony could hardly have expected.

He spoke of how the body is washed by two priests in bull's urine and water. And of how the mourners do not touch the corpse as they would be defiled by the decomposition which is the work of demons.

We can't even re-enter the room for ten days after the body has been removed. Fire is brought into the room to drive off corruption and disease and a couple of dogs to frighten off any demons. Dogs are spiritual beings.

Tony was in total awe.

So do you bury the body or cremate it?

Until the 1960's we did neither because we believe that the demons of death, which cause the body to rot, defile the fire and the earth which are both sacred.

So what did you do?

The priests removed the shroud with tools, tongs I guess you would say, to avoid touching the body and they returned home to wash themselves. The whole room was washed. The body was the taken to the Tower of Silence with all the mourners following in pairs.

Azad described the Tower of Silence.

It's like the turret of a castle, high in the sky. The body is left there alone to await the vultures.

Fucking hell Azad. I mean bloody heck Azad.

Once they come it does not take long; maybe five minutes and the dead flesh is gone.

That sounds fantastic. It all makes sense. Those ugly vulture bastards are probably demons anyway and they eat all the shit. Brilliant. And you're just left with the clean bones.

Yes we burn the clean bones or bury them.

And are you still able to do this?

Not anymore. But we hope to one day. These days we just use the cemetery or the crematorium.

Oh but a Tower of Silence would be so good. The vultures and all.

And reincarnation. You go for that Azad?

That's the Sikhs again.

Delgatty collected Higgins from the kennel and coated him up in the striped jacket of the six dog.

Evening Skinner. You were having a chat with Punch?

Yeah. He says I've got to wait for him here.

I would do then.

On the terrace in front of the bar the others shared the laughter and the relief as Higgins trapped clear and stayed there to win by five lengths in 16.80 over the sprint trip.

Delgatty picked the dog up at the brake and took him back to the paddock. He washed his feet meticulously and Punch lifted him on to the carpet behind the back seat of the Vauxhall and gently closed the hatch.

Can I go now Punch?

Course you can Skinner.

He handed Skinner nine five pound notes.

Oh thanks Punch. Cheers Mate.

You had a fiver at 5/1 and fifteen quid to come. For helping me look after the dog Skin. That's all.

Delgatty had witnessed Punch's diplomacy as he brought him a coke from the bar.

Blessed are the peacemakers.

Punch was pleased to sit with the dog.

You sure you're all right Punch. We could take him in the bar.

What with all that smoke?

Punch was very health conscious as a former athlete himself.

Or we could go to The Mulberry Tree.

No I want to sit and talk to him anyway.

The celebrating clique attracted all the attention in the bar that night as Delgatty wanted them to. So thank God for dog sitter Punch.

Tony was on some new medication and had decided to join Punch, Azad and Judge in staying teetotal but the others were watched drinking champagne and were the talk of the track.

They backed that off the boards at the last minute. 5/1 to odds on. That big bastard, looks like a wrestler, had two bets of a hundred quid.

Delgatty had given Punch the two hundred to place a bet. Punch put another tenner on for himself and Skinner. Delgatty asked Judge to put a further two hundred on. Judge had weighed in with a ton of his own. Tony, Father and Dexter had looked after their own bets as had the women. Esther Marie had found the courage to join the crowds in front of the bookmakers and she and Harriet had had twenty quid each on Higgins.

Thanks for ringing Delgatty. Thanks.

Judge stood with his cigarette in one hand and his orange juice in the other.

Laverman stood at the bar and watched them too. He'd taken eight hundred pounds of the gamble, a great deal of money for a small track, and he took the hit grudgingly. As Delgatty and his friends left the bar Father Ryan noticed Laverman signal Judge to join him.

What are those bastards up to?

The holy man spoke aloud to himself.

Hurricane had recovered quickly from the race and was showing no signs of blowing when Delgatty returned to the car.

Thanks Punch. We'll drop you home Mate.

It's OK Delgatty. Tony's giving me a lift.

Esther Marie, Harriet and Delgatty drove into the Staffordshire dark.

Well done boy.

Good boy.

They cooed alternately.

Next time there'll be nobody there except us two.

Three.

Harriet was starting to enjoy this dog lark.

Us three and Father Ryan. Nobody knows him round here. Higgins'll be in the first round of the Derby over the longer distance and they'll think we don't fancy him because the gang isn't there. And if I get it right Laverman will be on our side, just for this once.

Esther Marie was pensive.

I'm pretty sure Father Ryan must be recognised by now Jay. You've been seen with him on the train, in Ireland, Holyhead, Perry Barr for heaven's sake. You're going to have to get him to stay away for a while. And Skinner will be there. He always is you say. And won't Judge be there too? Have you thought this through Jay?

She was right.

29.

Get on your bed. Good lad.

Higgins' eyes blinked brightly from the straw in the darkness. It was the night after his win at Brownhills and Delgatty had given him an easy day, just a couple of road miles and a mooch around in the paddock for an hour.

There's a good boy. Good dogs. That's it for today.

Delgatty made sure all the doors were secure, locked the main kennel door and crossed the black drive to the house. The coffee percolator was coughing a light mist on to the curtainless kitchen windows.

Esther Marie shouted that she was in the bath.

OK I've just got to make a phone call. Come down when you're ready and we'll have a coffee.

He took the white business card that Laverman had given him at the races.

Mr. Cyril Laverman, Turf Accountant. There was a PO Box address and a Knowle phone number. Delgatty dialled. He held the card between finger and thumb and slanted his head as he read it again.

Hello Mr. Laverman. It's Delgatty. I thought you'd be back by now. I guessed you'd be at King's Heath this evening. Hope all the favourites didn't win.

I was wondering if we might have a chat. It's business. I've got an idea I'd like to run past you. Look you must've had enough for one day. Let's just say I'll be in The Fleece *at one o'clock tomorrow. OK leave it like that. See you then if you find you can make it.*

He flicked the card on to the window sill and put down the phone.

Esther Marie came into the room in her white dressing gown rubbing her wet hair with a towel.

Who was that?

Laverman. I was just setting up a meeting.

Setting up. *Good choice of words.*

Delgatty kissed her.

Let's sit either side of the fire. I'll get the coffee.

30.

Delgatty waited for Laverman in the bar of *The Golden Fleece*. He became fascinated by the pale eye shadow of the oriental barmaid. She spoke in perfect Black Country English.

What can Oi get for yow Sir?

Delagatty took his drink to a window table and looked out on to the street. Across the road was a junk shop with assorted bits of furniture and bric-a-brac on the pavement outside; an ottoman, a baby's high chair, a bike, a bookshelf with paperbacks and all that sort of stuff.

It had started to rain and the proprietor came out to rescue his merchandise. Delgatty became interested. He thought the guy would take the ottoman in first as it was upholstered and would spoil in the wet. Or maybe he would take the books. He didn't. He took the bike.

Delgatty assumed that the man had prioritised the bike as the most expensive item. That must be what he was doing. He was taking the dearest in first. Next he took a pedal car which Delgatty guessed was about the same value as the bike. The ottoman was last to go inside.

A man's voice interrupted Delgatty as he watched this little roadside drama.

I'm late Delgatty. I'll have what you're having as long as it's brandy with ice. One lump. Bloody demonstration in the middle of town. Load of unwashed communists. These strikers, miners, railway workers, will ruin the lot of us Delgatty.

Laverman swept into the bar in the company of one of his minders.

Delgatty made no response. He lived in the heart of the mining community and that's where his sympathies lay. He wouldn't be able to agree one single, political issue with Laverman so he got straight to the point.

I wanted to talk to you about my dog Higgins Mr. Laverman.

Didn't know you'd got a dog called Higgins. Is that Higgins as in the bullfighter?

No as in The Hurricane. Sorry I meant my dog Hurricane. Higgins is his kennel name.

O Alex.

Yes.

The thug removed his dark glasses, wiped his brow and grunted. He had a glass eye.

Good dog that.

Delgatty didn't respond but emptied his brandy glass. Laverman leant forward.

We took some stick on that Hurricane didn't we Slicer? About a grand wasn't it?

Delgatty imagined Slicer didn't get his name from working behind the bacon counter.

He looked at the burly, ugly frame of this rough, middle-aged bastard. His hair crept over his shirt collar and beyond his sleeves on to the back of his tattooed hands. His green, glass eye had been unsympathetically created by some 1950's Black Country quack and glared randomly around the room. The thug replaced his sunglasses and Delgatty felt the room dim slightly.

Definitely over a grand Boss.

Laverman looked impatiently at the clock behind the bar.

What's your deal Delgatty son? There's six meetings today and they'll run me skint if I'm not at the end of a phone. First race is in half an hour.

Well as your colleague has intimated this dog has class. He is the real deal. I've got him in the first round of The Cup the Monday after next.

I know when the bloody Cup is. I sponsor the fucking thing. Costs me money every year.

I'm just saying Mr. Laverman, I've paid the twenty quid entry fee and the racing manager was happy to accept him. He'll definitely win his heat. In fact I'd like you to back him as a sign of good faith on my part. He's only run in sprints at the track so we can't get a red light.

The red light was introduced into greyhound racing to help prevent cheating and to stop dogs winning by miles. You could find improvement of one second which was about twelve lengths but if the racing manager decreed a red light all bets were automatically void. If you'd never run over the trip though you couldn't get a red light as there were no figures to base it on.

You say he's only run in sprints in England. How do you know he won't need this first race over five hundred?

Oh I'll get a couple of gallops into him. I've got ten days or so.

He looked at his glass. Laverman called the girl.

Two more brandies. What you want?

Orange Boss.

The deal Mr. Laverman is The Cup.

Laverman had put the money up for The Brownhills Derby since its inception in 1971. It had come to be known locally as The Cup. The event, over five hundred yards, was for forty eight greyhounds in first round heats, quarters, semis and final and was run over two weeks. The prize of a thousand pounds to the winner competed with anything the bigger NGRC tracks could offer and was the permit trainers' blue riband. It was unusually early in the year for a classic race but it didn't lack interest from the greyhound community and was always oversubscribed.

After the first round Hurricane should head the market to win the whole thing.

Laverman looked at the clock again.

And you want me to lay him.

It wasn't a question.

Delgatty nodded.

Fifty fifty.

And you'll nail him.

To the ground.

Even though it was a lie Delgatty hated even the thought of such an abomination. Slicer cracked his face with something near a smile.

And I'm going to trust you to do that?

Yes.

Laverman stared for a long moment into the eyes of this confident man.

I'm not going to piss you about Delgatty. You were involved in that gamble at Wolverhampton. Judge told me. So in my book you owe me. You lot cost me a lot of money that day.

Delgatty knew this was a nut that had to be cracked.

I had no idea that I would end up backing that thing Mr. Laverman. I just followed the money in. Pure luck.

Yes, well. It was a bad business all round.

Delgatty in mid-swallow almost spat out his drink but composed himself. A bad business? So that's what they call murder these days.

Laverman started to get up.

No. I don't like the sound of it.

Hold on a minute Boss.

Slicer was an opportunist. He would never qualify for a bookmaker's licence himself with, what one imagined, was a criminal past but he was not averse to putting money in the bag on occasions. If you put money in a bookmaker's bag for a particular race, you made the profit or stood the loss on the whole event or you could opt to lay just one horse or dog and win or lose on the performance of that one animal. This was only ever done by the consent of the bookmaker of course and bordered on illegal, unlicensed betting.

You can back and lay it to your heart's content, Slicer. I'm having none of it.

Slicer stood to leave with his gaffer and turned to Delgatty.

OK we'll lay sixes and sevens and you nail him in the first round. Job done.

No.

Slicer sat down again. Delgatty was insistent.

Mr. Slicer, the serious betting won't start till the first two rounds are over.

Hold on there Delgatty. You taking the piss? Don't call me Slicer and definitely don't call me Mr. Slicer. My name is Waterson.

Sorry Mr. Waterson, that was presumptuous of me.

Delgatty thought to himself that Slicer must be his kennel name.

What I was going to say was I'll stop him in the semis. We'll take five times as much and he might get knocked out before then anyway. He'd have to fall over but it could happen.

And how much do you think we'll take on the dog?

That Mr. Waterson is where I have to trust you.

Fair enough. If the dog wins in the first round we'll talk again only I'm not promising. We might only get a few hundred apiece out of it. The Cup's worth a grand. Why not go for that?

Too uncertain. I'm in a bit of bother for cash.

What after that Wolverhampton touch?

I just paid out a lot of money for the dog Mr. Waterson.

Delgatty shrugged. Waterson grinned toothily.

You dog men. Always in a bit of trouble. I understand you've got a reputation in the dog world Delgatty. Judge says you always run 'em straight. Seems you're as bent as the rest of 'em.

That wounded Delgatty.

Laverman was impatient to leave. He got up and swallowed his drink, crunching the last dregs of ice. Delgatty rose too and reached for his back pocket.

Before you go. Here's my money for Monday. I'm not telling anyone else to back it. You should get a good price.

He pulled out five hundred pounds in battered fivers and tenners from his inside pocket and offered them to Laverman.

Don't give it me. Your business is with Slicer.

Waterson took the cash. Laverman headed for the door.

Come on. Let's go see what sort of a bloody mess they're getting me in.

When the two men had left the lounge Delgatty shuddered like he was shaking off the lies he had necessarily told and leaned his elbows on the bar. He spoke to the barmaid.

I feel like celebrating. Let me buy you a drink.

Half an hour later he left the pub and called in at the shop across the road. He bought a Wedgwood vase decorated with Greek Gods for Esther Marie and as he paid for it he asked the man how he decided what to bring in first when it started raining.

It's just the way it fits in the shop. Bring it in any other way and it won't fit.

Tony would have loved to have been there to have seen further evidence for his theory that no man can be sure of another's thinking.

31.

For the remainder of the week Delgatty worked hard on Higgins. He did five miles of fast roadwork each morning and spent an hour a day grooming and massaging the dog. The fact that he was coming to hand showed in the dog's coat and his readiness to work and he really needed a strenuous five hundred yard plus trial to pull him out in preparation for the stiffer trip of The Cup. There was nothing to give him a proper trial at the permit track and anyway Delgatty didn't want to further expose the dog's talents to the watchers there.

I think Queenie would lead him, Marie. What do you think?

Yes if she trapped level she'd lead him for a couple of hundred yards.

Queenie, whose NGRC registered name was Atalanta, was the track record holder over two hundred and sixty five yards at 15.19 seconds at Brownhills and although sprinting was her forte she did actually stay five two five yards and had won over that trip several times so she wouldn't be daunted. In fact she had clocked 29.83 at Perry Barr at just two years of age when Delgatty had entrusted her for a couple of months to an NGRC trainer he respected.

She hasn't seemed to worry about her shoulder?

She's showing no signs of a problem, walks sound. She's not dropping on it and she's done everything Higgins has done in roadwork so she's fit enough.

So it was to be a match between the two of them; a private match with no unwelcome watchers. And there was only one place for that to take place, Kidderminster.

Delgatty had decided to take the opportunity to give the two young dogs a trial as well in the company of old Rex.

Just before dawn Delgatty and Esther Marie pulled onto the M1 at Exit 30 near Sheffield. The five dogs were restless in the back of the estate; the senior animals knowing that a chase lay ahead of them. Delgatty murmured reassuringly to the muzzled creatures.

Delgatty and Esther Marie were on their way to Kidderminster.

As they drove past Exit 29 their attention was taken by a flock of Canada Geese in the half-light flying from right to left across the motorway only about one hundred feet above them.

I wonder if one gave the signal to move on or if they all decided in their automatic pea-brains at the same instant to take off.

Delgatty knew where they were going. There are five small lakes on the Hewett estate and the birds come and go according to their own goosey agenda. A few minutes later they witnessed the whole thing over again. Another flock in similarly ragged formation crossed above them.

It's as if the earth is turning like some gigantic combination lock and we are keeping up with it in this old Vauxhall.

He warmed to Esther Marie's treatise.

The cogs click into place and the parallel tiny combinations in the birds' skulls click too. These geese are responding like automatons to the revolutions of dark and light. The same scene will be being repeated the length and breadth of the country.

The world outpaced them, however, and the remainder of the trip was goose free.

Esther Marie enjoyed these philosophical exchanges with her brother. It reminded her of meals at home when her mum and dad were alive. Politics, art, science and religion had been as important as the food on the table. She put a hand on his knee.

I need a coffee. You want some?

She took a flask out of her bag. The steam from the coffee merged with the smell of the dogs' breath and the liniment.

They arrived at the Kidderminster trial track just before nine o'clock. The dogs were pacing the back of the car with anticipation, steaming up the rear windows with their hot breath. Even though the sun was only watery Delgatty parked in the shade and went to the wooden shed where the entries were taken.

The track at Kidderminster did not stage actual races but provided a schooling track for saplings. Most importantly it was used by trainers and handlers to run their dogs unofficially and to get a gallop into them before a key public appearance. Delgatty would know that morning how much progress his Cup dog was making. The electronic timing at the track would give him an accurate picture. A very good greyhound would cover the five hundred and twenty five yards in about 31.50 seconds. Kidderminster was a very stiff galloping track. Brownhills was much faster and twenty five yards shorter. 31.50 here was equivalent to about 29.60 there.

The pups had already had a couple of handslips. The slipper, Delgatty in this case, usually stands about fifty yards from the bend and releases the dog as the hare passes. Two bends is enough at this early stage.

Delgatty had put them through the trap he had at home to acclimatise them. He would put the young animals in the back of the trap gently and without fuss, leave them a couple of minutes, spring the front open and they would emerge in modes of excitement or relief. Later he brought out the drag hare, which looked like a dusty wig flitting across the turf. It was powered by an old starter motor and the saplings loved to chase this bit of rag in the field next to the house.

He had taken them to the local flapping track at Chesterfield and given them each a solo trial around two bends and they had both chased the hare convincingly so he thought they were ready for their first trial in the company of other dogs, always a tricky affair.

He had decided to run the two young dogs with Rex. The old dog was pretty fit from roadwork and he would teach the pups how to chase and manage the bends. Rex would love to beat them being an old pro. He was utterly genuine and would run straight and true. The worst could happen with the pups, of course, and they could lose interest in the hare or get unsighted and start to mess around, playing or fighting with each other; the biggest crimes a greyhound can commit.

Delgatty imagined Bobby and Frankie would steer a wide course and the last thing he wanted was for trouble at the bend. Rex was inclined to rail but might well run to the middle as he had been off the track for so long. So the plan was to run Rex from Trap 2 and

Frankie and Bobby from Traps 4 and 6.

The ground was a little on the slow side. The times of the other dogs which were already trialling were not publicly announced. To preserve the secrecy of the trial you had to report to the judge's box to get your time but Delgatty got a good impression from his own hand-timing of the first dozen or so trials. Most appeared to be moderate animals going round in about 32.50. Of course he did not know how good these anonymous dogs were but he knew one or two of the faces with them and he could tell a dog that was racing. To the experienced eye there is a world of difference between a dog undergoing serious work to one still short of its best.

Delgatty recognised the head lad to one of the trainers at a Birmingham track installing a big fawn dog in a middle trap for a solo. The dog raced impressively, without checking, and Delgatty clocked it at 31.67. Two more dogs from the same source returned times of 31.85 and 32.15. It wasn't much to go on but suggested, unless these dogs were open race class, that the track was running about standard.

He returned to the car as the tannoy asked for dogs numbered 23, 24 and 25 for the sprint trip which were Rex and the pups. Delgatty had asked for a breathing space before Hurricane and Queenie ran and they were numbered 36 and 37.

Esther Marie held on to the leads of Higgins and Queenie whilst Delgatty got the pups and Rex out of the back of the car. Once she had lifted her two charges back into the car and the hatch was shut she joined Delgatty and took Rex's lead. They approached the traps at the sprint start and held on to the dogs in the middle of the track.

When the trial before theirs was over and the runners had been caught, Esther Marie deftly slipped Rex into the two box and held Frankie whilst Delgatty lifted Bobby wholesale into Trap 5 and shut the back. Esther Marie went round the front of the traps to check all was well and Delgatty loaded Frankie into the six box. He waved OK to the hare driver and the two of them stepped back. The hare sped past and tripped the lids.

Frankie broke pretty much on terms with old Rex. Bobby missed the start by about ten lengths but at least both pups were out and chasing.

Go on Rex old lad.

Rex asserted at the first bend where Frankie checked and ran wide. Bobby was charting a middle course eight lengths behind. Frankie got to Rex's quarters at the second and final bend only to lose ground again. By the time they got to the line Frankie had got Rex's measure and, to Delgatty's delight and mixed feelings for Esther Marie, went by straight as a dart to win by a length. Rex had a couple of lengths in hand of Bobby.

Brilliant run from Frankie but they both ran true enough.

Delgatty shouted to Esther Marie, resolving to give them solo runs next time to confirm and hopefully cement their desire to chase.

That old boy of yours ran a blinder!

A pleasing starter was followed by the main course over the full five hundred and twenty five yards. Esther Marie held the other dogs whilst Delgatty got Queenie and Higgins from the back of the car.

We'll wash all their feet on the way out.

The taps were just by the entrance to the track.

Esther Marie lifted Queenie gently into Trap 3, not ideal for her as she did tend to run a little wide but they fully expected her to lead her younger opponent in Trap 6. The hare sped past and the two dogs broke on terms. Queenie led by a length at the first bend but Higgins was already on her shoulder as they turned into the back straight and pulled clear for a decisive five length win. Delgatty had the time at 31.10, a superb performance by both dogs.

Esther Marie arrived breathlessly at the brake, empathising with Queenie in her moment of defeat.

I hope we haven't broken her heart Jay.

Of course not Marie. We'll give her a sprint next week and she'll be right as rain.

Delgatty was in truth cock-a-hoop with Higgins' run but he

wouldn't disappoint Queenie for the world. She wouldn't mind. The bitch would know she'd needed a blow.

Delgatty called in the wooden office to confirm both race times. They had Hurricane at 31.20 which was fine and the pup had turned in a time of 19.50 for two hundred and sixty five yards which was fine too.

Bloody hell. I don't know which of them I'm more pleased with!

They got the bucket from the car and washed all the dogs' feet in the small concrete paddock at the entrance to the track.

As they pulled away, the dogs safely stowed in the back of the Vauxhall, unknown to them, a tall delicate man emerged from the trees on the far side of the course. He checked his stop watch and wrote something in biro on the back of his hand. It was Judge.

32.

Claudia are you in the kitchen?

He pronounced *Claudia* in the Italian and to the untutored ear it was close to *Cloudier.*

It was Saturday night and Waterson had just dropped Laverman at his house in Knowle. Having looked in the lounge for his wife, he shouted up the stairs.

Claudia are you up there?

He went back into the room, poured himself a brandy from the decanter and sat down in his arm chair. He heard light footsteps on the stairs and his wife appeared in her dressing gown.

I was asleep. You're late.

Yes the bloody night lark has started already. Windsor on the blower and about ten men in the shop. Four bloody favourites went in. Everyone of 'em drawn high in a sprint. Multiply that by six shops. You've got no chance running a book at a track like that.

Well why don't you sell up, retire? Hills and Ladbrokes are always looking for chains of shops. We could do so much together. Let's go back to Italy.

I couldn't retire. What would I do? Come and arrange flowers at church with you on a Saturday afternoon. It's in my blood this game.

She poured herself a small brandy and sat on the large, high-back, white, leather sofa, patting the space beside her. Laverman rose, took off his coat which he chucked in the chair he had just vacated. He topped up his drink and sat next to his wife.

It's not just the game Cyril. It's everything that goes with it. You mix with some unpleasant people and you're not an unpleasant person.

Tell me about it. That Waterson is a bleeding psychopath. He's a law to himself. I told him to stay out of that bother at Wolverhampton the other day. OK it cost us a lot of money but I said we should just leave it. Take it on the chin. Next thing an old man's dead and he says he knows nothing about it. I have my suspicions but what can I do?

Sack him. You're the boss.

O yeah. You know him do you Claudia? He's a bleeding nutcase.

Why don't you talk to the police?

Police? Are you mad? Once you involve them your life is never your own. I just want to get on with what I'm good at - well not so good at tonight - laying horses and dogs and running the casino. It's all pretty straight forward and legal.

That's just broken my dream Cyril. Just now before you came home I dreamt you were involved in something very big and very troubling and I saw another death. It was awful; a death by hanging.

It's just a dream, a bit of nonsense Claudia.

He laughed as he recollected his meeting with Delgatty.

I did get asked to get into a bit of a dodgy deal last Saturday. Bloke wanted me to lay his dog and he's going to stop it winning. I told him I wasn't interested. Waterson wants to put the money up for it though. That's his business.

He rose to refill both their glasses.

I will retire in a couple of years and we'll disappear into the Italian sunset. In the meantime whatever Waterson gets up to I don't want anything to do with it.

33.

The night Hurricane ran for Waterson's money, only Delgatty and Esther Marie were there apart from Punch who was sitting on watch outside the kennel; sitting on the lucky canvas stool. Delgatty had taken Esther Marie's advice and asked Father Ryan, Tony and the others to absent themselves on this occasion. Azad was working anyway. He'd got a rare fare to Heathrow and it was Harriet's turn to look after her own and the refugee kids.

Skinner was there of course. He was dipping into a bag of pork scratchings as he approached Delgatty's table and spat small fragments as he spoke.

You not fancy your dog tonight then Delgatty?

Not sure if he'll get the trip on this ground Skinner.

He got it round Clonmel didn't he?

You had to admire Skinner's retention for detail of a dog's form.

He's 5/2 out there.

Well back him if you like Skinner. We'll just watch him tonight. That was good fast ground at Clonmel. This is a bit sticky tonight. Times seem slow.

Skinner tipped the last of the scratchings into his mouth and screwed the empty packet impolitely into Delgatty's ash tray. He left the bar and headed for the ring where he would no doubt pass on the information he had just secured from Delgatty.

Mannerless oaf. You wouldn't think he'd want any more scratchings though would you?

That's unkind Jay. He might just help us with the price when he tells the bookies what you said about Higgins' chance.

It was unkind of me. You're right as always Marie. We've got five hundred quid to the odds so that'll do. Laverman and Waterson will probably push the price out anyway. We might get a couple of grand out of it.

Delgatty suddenly noticed Judge at the bar with one of Laverman's heavies.

What is he doing here? Marie can you keep an eye on him outside and see what he does. I'll go and get the dog ready.

Delgatty walked out to the paddock.

Everything OK Punch?

Yeah fine Delgatty. Nobody's been near.

Delgatty collected Higgins and coated him up in the orange five jacket, slipping the wire racing muzzle over his snout and anchoring the buckled, leather straps behind his ears. He walked the dog through the gate on to the middle of the track and paraded Higgins in numerical order with the five others.

Punch wandered back into the betting ring and joined Esther Marie. They saw Judge about to hand over a small wad of cash to one of the bookies. He spoke involuntarily, remembering Delgatty wanted none of the gang to be involved this time.

Don't back it Judge.

But Judge did back it. And he backed it again and again down the line and the dog's price contracted to odds on.

Hurricane shot out of the traps and was never headed to win his heat by eight lengths in a new track record of 29.33 seconds.

Delgatty handed the lead and the car keys to Punch when he had finished washing Higgins' feet and had wiped him down. Delgatty was elated with his dog's performance but was undemonstrative in front of the small group who had assembled at the paddock side.

Skinner leaned on the paddock railings.

You think he stays the trip now Delgatty? Fucking 'ell. He could've gone round again.

Delgatty only smiled in reply and spoke to Punch instead.

I've just got to have a word with someone. We'll be out in a minute. We'll have a drink at The Mulberry Tree *on the way home.*

Waterson was at the bar with Laverman.

There's a grand there Delgatty. 5/4 on it finished and you got even money to your monkey. Sorry that's all but it's a bastard when your price goes.

Delgatty took the money unflinchingly. He knew Waterson was referring to his own and Laverman's fury at the price of News from Thebes.

That's fine Mr. Waterson. A thousand pounds is a lot of money. Thanks

Waterson moved closer to Delgatty and spoke into his ear.

OK I'll go along with it. One more round then you stop the dog. Don't screw up.

Delgatty nodded and Waterson drew back.

You want a drink Delgatty?

No thanks. We're off to The Mulberry Tree. It's a sort of tradition to go there after racing. It's on our way home.

Esther Marie was waiting for him in the car park.

To hell with Laverman and Waterson.

Yes to hell with them. How much did we win?

A monkey.

That's OK. Five hundred quid is fine.

I'm not sure who is the real boss in that outfit. That Waterson seems to have a big say in what goes on.

Delgatty spotted the lean figure of Judge bending himself into his aubergine mini.

Oi Judge what were you doing? I thought we'd agreed we left the dog alone tonight. Oi Judge I'm talking to you.

Judge stood up again, one foot in the well of the car.

Oh for fuck's sake Delgatty. Think about it.

Delgatty approached Judge.

Think about what?

By now a small crowd had begun to assemble. Laverman himself was approaching the edge of it.

Delgatty calm down.

But he would not calm down and took a swing at Judge and quickly found himself held by one of Laverman's thugs.

Judge shook his head with embarrassment, climbed back into his J Registration car, keyed the engine into life and laboured, in second gear, across the uneven cinders to the exit. The watchers-on dispersed muttering to each other. Laverman frowned to himself.

OK we'll tell Judge nothing in future, Marie. OK? Nothing. To hell with him.

OK. To hell with him too.

They both laughed, joined Punch in the car with Hurricane, and drove to *The Mulberry Tree*.

34.

Delgatty's dream that night found him in open countryside. It was an idyllic scene and the sun was so hot he knelt down at a shallow stream to quench himself. His blurred image in the moving water seemed to exaggerate the size of his eyes as he drank directly from the beck.

There were cries in the distance as if people were calling to each other. He walked away from the noise but the shouts grew louder and he began to feel they were directed at him. He tried to shout back but no sound came from him. He could not clear his mind to think. He could not really think.

The shouting increased and now Delgatty could make out flags being waved by the line of men and women who appeared to be following him. He sensed this advancing file was hostile to him and moved more quickly until he arrived at a large grassy sward. He could see in the distance hundreds of people standing on a green embankment to the right of him and at the edge of the field to his left and he recognised the place as Withins Field.

His hearing seemed to be enhanced and amongst the babble of the crowd he could single out a voice he knew.

Where is Delgatty? Surely he's not going to miss Higgins and Queenie. There's a hare on the edge of the field now.

He's probably waiting at the bottom of the field to pick the dogs up after the course. Don't worry he'll be here somewhere. Oh look there's Judge.

The voices were those of Mary and Tony.

Look at Judge.

Judge came into Delgatty's focus bedecked in full hunting red, sitting astride his horse, waiting for a hare to enter the arena. The hack pranced impatiently under restraint as the pristine galloping surface invited him to show his paces.

Delgatty heard Mary again,

Yes and doesn't Dexter look fine? Where's Penny by the way?

She said she would come later.

Delgatty heard the voice of Dexter and he too zoomed into view as happens in dreams. The red-jacketed Dexter stood in the shy with Delgatty's two greyhounds in his slips.

Steady yaw two. That old hare's on his way. Steady nah.

As his dream-director panned the crowd, Diana, the beautiful Diana, appeared in sudden, sharp focus, watching silently and impassively from the top of the bank.

Delgatty stamped his hind feet in rage at the danger he was in. Surely they could see it was himself and not a hare. He looked down at the fur on his bare trembling feet. His wide eyes rotated in his head.

He thought he could see the back of the shy so maybe it was not too late to turn back but the way was blocked by the beaters whose noise was now deafening to him and he would be better going forward.

He would have to take his chance on what he now knew was the running ground. He had wits. He was a man and not a hare. Surely his wits were superior to those of two dogs. He tried to think but panic was swamping his thoughts. He felt claustrophobic in the head of the hare like Jesus Christ crammed into the mind of a man.

Think man, think! A hare can….a hare can…..a hare can make 45 mph.

His brain found some fluency.

The top burst of a hare is 45 mph. A greyhound can do just under 40 mph. The hare makes its dash too early. I need to conserve energy to make it to the reeds.

He moved on in small skips until the shy, despite its green camouflage, came into clear view. The crowd and the beaters were now silent.

I must get to the very edge of the shy before sprinting. I'll get a hundred yards on them. I can make it.

When he thought he had reached the optimum point on the field Delgatty started to break into a run. After five strides he was in full flight heading towards the rhododendrons with five hundred, four hundred, three hundred yards to go. He was dully aware of the shouts in the crowd urging on his pursuers; his own beloved Hurricane and Atalanta, his friends Higgins and Queenie.

Even though he had only fifty yards to go he knew he could not make it and was forced to make a turn, Queenie's jaws snapped and missed as he cut back towards the centre of the field and twisted and turned his way to the bottom of the bank where he had once, as a man, witnessed a hare make a daring escape.

I think Queenie has the edge on Higgins in this one. I hope Delgatty isn't missing this.

Tony nodded his agreement with Mary.

Delgatty started his slalom run up the hill but Higgins it was who put his teeth into his shoulder and threw him on his back. Queenie dived in for the kill and he felt his head being crushed by her jaws as Tony was quickly on the scene separating the two dogs and dispatching Delgatty with a swift rabbit punch. Hares don't usually make sounds but in such extremis they have been known to let out an ungodly scream and Delgatty did so now.

Well done Tony darling. I hate to see them suffer.

Delgatty saw the whole of Withins Field as if in a film. The final act before the curtain of his sleeping life was drawn back was to see Judge raising his hunting hat as if in reverence but, according to the rules of the course, he was actually signalling a draw between the red and white collars of Hurricane and Atalanta.

He woke to the swish of Esther Marie drawing back the curtains.

You scared me Jay. You were screeching. Are you OK?

He told her about the nightmare. She considered his words.

Oh I see. Have you been looking at naked women?

She was half scolding, half teasing in her tone.

Delgatty sat up in bed, speechless after the nightmare.

Esther Marie grew more teacher-like.

Actaeon?

Who?

Actaeon came across Diane or was it Diana? I can't remember. Anyway it was one or the other and her nymphs bathing naked and the goddess changed him into a stag and hunted him to death with his own hounds. It's in Ovid.

O yeah I remember. Yeah I remember. It was Diana.

And the naked women?

Delgatty reached for the tea Esther Marie had placed by the side of the bed.

Naked women? Nah.

35.

By the night of the quarter finals of The Cup, there were just twenty four dogs in four heats. Laverman and his sidekick had a problem. Obviously they expected Higgins to win his heat but having agreed that Delgatty was going to stop the dog in the semi-finals they wanted to bet against Higgins winning the event outright. Waterson wrestled with the problem.

I reckon you should put up 4/9 for the heat and evens for the final, Boss.

Ok. It's your money.

Laverman took quite a few bets at even money, including a couple of hundred quid from a smartly dressed couple he had never seen before.

A hundred pounds on that Ev thing please.

Conrad was referring to the way Laverman had chalked up Hurricane at Ev for even money.

A hundred pounds on that Ev thing please.

Conrad put the ticket in his coat pocket and wiped his hands on a scarlet handkerchief. Yoko did the same on her own, identical, scarlet handkerchief.

Father Ryan had independently decided that 4/9 was a good price for the heat and bet ninety pounds of his own money to win forty. He was right and Hurricane brushed aside the opposition with ease, leading from trap to line in just five spots off the track record. Ryan calculated that forty pounds would pay for a couple of coach trips for the parish's two under-eighteen rugby teams.

36.

You can't swallow a frog by looking at it.

Father Ryan had once shared this adage with Delgatty who knew that the night of the semi-finals was the frog that had to be swallowed.

It was the night that Waterson would know for certain he had been set up and the night Delgatty and his friends would take an irrevocable step towards avenging the ill-fated Cadman. It was the night that Waterson might decide to eat him alive.

Higgins was in the second heat and Delgatty had him at the track in plenty of time.

He looks fuckin' fantastic, Delgatty. Ready to run for his life.

Punch marched his huge body into the paddock, swinging his collapsible, canvas stool in one hand.

Delgatty checked the racing kennel was clean, put the dog inside and left Punch to keep guard. He climbed the short run of steps up to the nearside of the bar and lit a cigar before entering. The tannoy asserted that the runners for the first semi-final were on parade.

What you fancy in this heat, Delgatty?

I think the bitch Nemesis must have a strong chance, Skinner. Excuse me I've got to get back to the paddock in a minute and just want to check on my sisters.

Yes I like Nemesis too. Good luck with yours anyway. Laverman's going even money for the final. Looks a big price to me.

It will be if he wins tonight.

Delgatty made his way to the corner of the bar where his sisters and friends had managed to group an assortment of chairs and bar stools into a circle.

This is it then.

He nodded at each of them.

Where's Judge?

I think he's outside. He hasn't spoken to us yet. Too busy studying this first heat I expect.

And Penny? Coming later I suppose?

Mary smiled.

Right, I'd better go and watch it too.

Delgatty was clearly nervous and probably as scared as he'd ever been.

Nemesis was favourite for the first semi-final at around 5/4 and she lived up to her price by winning readily. She had looked in trouble, having been baulked at the first bend, but quickly regained her equilibrium to put in a storming late run and pull a couple of lengths clear of her field at the line to win in 29.50 seconds. Delgatty was impressed.

Higgins was in Trap 4 for his semi-final, not ideal as there were three wide runners in the race and he had the worst of the draw. Delgatty went to the racing office, picked up the black jacket and met Waterson on his way to the parade ring.

Been a lot of money for your dog Delgatty.

Oh that's good Mr. Waterson. Good.

You'd better not be putting me away, Delgatty.

Delgatty seemed not to hear and walked on to the paddock. Waterson stood still for a moment and you could almost hear his whirring thought-processes. He turned and hesitated before returning to the betting ring.

Laverman was laying Hurricane at 10/11 for this heat and had now reduced the odds for the final to 4/5 at Waterson's bidding. Laverman was growing more impatient by the minute.

I'll be glad when this race is over. Keep changing your fucking mind.

Delgatty's friends stayed in the bar until the announcement was made that the start was imminent. Not one of them had had a bet that night. They would not bet again until the cat was out of the bag, the worms had come pouring from the can and the excrement had hit the air conditioning.

Waterson had made a decision. Another decision.

Here you are Evens Hurricane!

A final few punters dashed in and took Laverman's generous price, seconds before the dogs sped from the traps. These dogs were the best of their breed. They were awesome in their paces, casting elongated electric shadows on the dark, green turf.

Higgins was, however, their imperious master and he made every yard of the running to win in 29.37, just four spots outside his own track record.

Delgatty had expected some immediate repercussions. He had at least expected Waterson to approach him or threaten him or take a swing at him. But nothing happened.

The rest of the group left the track unmolested too.

He washed Higgins' feet in the paddock whilst Punch stood with him but even here nobody approached other than friendly faces to congratulate him.

They seem to have taken that well then Delgatty?

For now Punch. For now. But we do have a problem.

What?

Higgins has cut a toe. I don't think it's broken but it's a nasty knock.

The boxer peered over his shoulder.

Just broken the skin I think but it'll be bruised. And we've only got a week.

Always something ain't there Delgatty?

37.

The cut on Hurricane's toe was not bad, not bad under normal circumstances, but it must be sore and would cost him a valuable length or so at the bends.

We'll have to see the man.

Delgatty picked up the phone and carried it over to his chair by the fire. The plastic cord stretched taut across the room. He dialled and waited, perched on the front of his seat.

Hello it's Delgatty. I've got a dog in a stake. It's the final in a week and he's got a cut. Can I come up tomorrow? It really is very urgent.

He turned to Esther Marie.

She's gone to ask him. He's operating.

After a four minute wait he got his answer.

Yes thank you. Ten o'clock tomorrow. Thanks.

At six that morning Delgatty put Higgins in the back of the estate. He caught Esther Marie's old black dog Rex, who was stretching his legs in the paddock and put him into his kennel with Queenie to await their return. As he locked the door, the dogs whined briefly.

On yer beds!

The whining stopped. The old dog stood looking silently at the door. He turned two or three times on the sawdust floor before collapsing with a sigh. Queenie had once again claimed the straw and the bed.

Nearly four hours later Delgatty and Marie arrived at Dalgleish's place just outside Glenrothes.

Radio 4 boomed continuously in the surgery as had its predecessor The Home Service a few years earlier. Delgatty remembered being there several times with a lead sheet over his groin, holding a dog whilst Dalgleish took Xrays from the safety of the corridor. The man was incredible. People came from all over Britain. Most vets were a waste of time to the greyhound community, especially the poodle vets in the town.

Yes Madam. Keep him warm. I've given him a penicillin injection. If he's not better in a week bring him back and I'll charge you another fifteen quid.

Most dogs get better in a week .

Doctors are the same, most of them. Six of them in a surgery so plenty of time for golf and people, like poodles, get better in a week.

This man was different. He was patience and he was almost magic but his feet were on the greyhound ground.

With one of these toe injuries I usually say three weeks. They can be nasty. How much is the prize money?

A grand but there's a lot more at stake than that.

Aye well you'll have to run him won't you? Let's see what we can do. You may have to bring him back to me afterwards but I think we can patch him up for one more race, then you really will have to rest him for a month if you don't want to fuck him up completely. He'll have to wear a bucket collar for the rest of the week to stop him messing with it.

An hour later he accompanied Esther Marie and Delgatty to the car park.

Now you pay no attention to it. It'll help him forget it if he thinks you're not worried. I've left it unbandaged. He's got a bit of a headache at the moment but that will pass.

A bit of a headache?

Esther Marie laughed in the car as they left.

If he says he's got a headache, he's got a bloody headache.

It was teatime when the estate car bounced back into the uneven driveway and pulled up short of the open garage doors. Their two doors opened simultaneously and the couple emerged stretching for relief after the trip.

I'll get us something to eat. What do you fancy?

Anything. Do me a favour. Just open the kennel door for me Marie.

Get your old lad out before you go in the house. You can leave him off in the garden. You know what he's like. He must be bursting for a piss.

Delgatty picked Higgins up from the back of the car and carried him to the door of the kennels.

Esther Marie reached for the key under the stone but immediately saw that the door was already ajar and the centre window was smashed. She gaped and stared.

Jay, the window's broken.

He put Higgins back in the car and closed the hatch. The dog leaned his bucketed head on one side in a gesture of puzzlement.

Esther Marie peered through the broken pane into the dim interior. Delgatty flung the door fully open. At first he could not see him but then he did.

Rex was suspended from a meat hook in the roof of the kennel by a single piece of cord wrapped round his hock and he turned slowly thus as if on a vertical spit. His throat had been cut. The sawdust below him was like crimson snow. Their eyes froze at the sight, neither moving nor speaking. The throat gaped at them.

Higgins issued a muffled bark from the car and the other dogs, witnesses all to this foul act, relieved at the break in the silence barked too. Delgatty was stirred into numbed action. He opened Higgins' kennel door and put Queenie inside.

Esther Marie turned her head away as he lifted the corpse from its hanging place and laid it on the bed.

Delgatty cut the heel of his hand on the meat hook and his blood commingled with the congealed blood of Rex.

That night Delgatty cleaned the kennels from top to bottom and buried Esther Marie's dog in the garden. He had only ever had to bury one other dog and that was Ruby Tuesday who had died peacefully and now lay under the turf of the vicarage garden. He covered the animal with earth and banged the turf back flat with the spade.

Those stupid bastards thought Rex was Hurricane. They can't tell a two year old dog from a retired greyhound. A black dog's a black dog. They probably wouldn't have noticed if he had been a labrador. If he'd been Boffy's dog.

He banged the spade again and wiped his eyes on his sleeve.

Esther Marie stayed in the house. Bob Dylan blasted from the stereo as she cooked furiously in the kitchen.

*He jumped so high, he jumped so high,
Then he lightly touched down,
Mr Bojangles, Mr Bojangles.*

The lyrics made her weep even more.

She had wanted to call the police but Delgatty wouldn't have it. There was only one thing to do and that was to win The Cup. Later as they opened a second bottle of wine Delgatty came to a unilateral policy decision.

Marie, we can tell the others about Rex but I don't want Judge to be told.

OK.

She handed him a mug.

What's this?

It's an infusion of herbs. It'll help you sleep after all the trauma of today.

OK. Mind if I stick a brandy in it?

38.

On the night of the final although the rain had stopped, the wind blew the leaves around Delgatty's paddocks and it was still very cold for late spring. He finished the last massage and stood back from the dog. Higgins remained with his front feet on the grooming stool. The sharpness of the liniment stung Delgatty's nose as he rubbed the towel once more down the length of the animal's back to remove the odd piece of scale.

You're a work of art you are boy.

Higgins, taking these words as confirmation that the session was over, stood down and shook himself.

Esther Marie had gone in Harriet's car and the others would already have set off for the track. Delgatty and the dog could not be there before the remaining money was down.

Azad had arrived early and the first person he had seen was Father Ryan in the bar.

Azad I presume. I'm glad you are here. Glad you are here Azad.

Thank you Father. Father Ryan. Delgatty told me about you. Good to see you. I've missed the last couple of meetings through bloody business but I believe the dog is running well.

The two men in white and black shook hands.

Zoroastrian then?

Yes Father Ryan.

Delgatty told me about you too and I've been doing some research Azad. We're not a million miles apart on what we believe are we? Apart from the vulture thing. Tony told me about that and wants it introducing into the Catholic rites. I can't see it going down too well in Birmingham or Cork.

There's always Dudley Zoo Father.

Both men laughed.

I see your Zarethrustra was born of a virgin some few hundred years before our Jesus.

Yes and we reckon your wise men were of our bloody lot.

And you're not alone in thinking that Azad. We have some scholars with that view in our own church.

One thing I must say Father. The dog is very important to us and it is an obligation to protect it and care for it.

Quite right.

And to kill a dog is to damn one's soul. Delgatty told me about Rex.

Well I understand what you are saying Azad but I'm never so quick to condemn anyone's soul. I'll leave that judgement to the one and just God.

He crossed himself.

Father we believe that we judge ourselves on the last day. We reach the Bridge of Judgement three days after we die and we decide which path to take.

Judge yourselves you say? I'll have to think about that one anyway.

39.

Waterson, believing Higgins to be dead, knew that he could not possibly run. He would still have to put up a price for the dog; not to do so would be tantamount to admitting his part in the muderous crime. He expected the announcement of a withdrawl and to have to refund all stakes bet on the dog on the night of the final. The five grand or so bet on the dog before final night would stay in the bag. They were ante-post wagers and would be lost when Higgins failed to materialise.

Delgatty and Higgins needed to be there for eight; the final was at nine. He put the bucket back round the dog's head. The toe had scabbed up well in the few days since the injury and he didn't want him chewing it now. He opened the internal kennel door.

Good lad then. Get on your bed. Dinner will be late tonight. Late for all of you.

He couldn't feed the other three without feeding Higgins. The dogs whined lightly as Delgatty switched off the light and locked the main door. He stood outside the kennels in the dark until he heard the collective rustle in the straw which meant they were lying back down. These dogs were so utterly patient. Delgatty walked back up the path to the house to get himself ready. It was gone six o'clock and he would have to leave by half past.

40.

In the stadium bar the portly, overcoated figure of Father Ryan moved across the carpet to Tony and Punch. Azad joined them. The four men shook hands.

It's a terrible thing that happened to the poor, old dog. They'll be paying for that tonight they will.

The priest nodded to the other three.

And for Terry Cadman.

Oh of course Punch. Of course. That was insensitive of me. The life of a man for God's sake.

He put his hand on the boxer's shoulder.

Tony put his hand in his pocket.

What will you have Father? Azad?

Ryan had a half of bitter and so did Azad. It didn't really matter now that the men should be seen together. They had between them betting receipts worth nearly ten thousand pounds, and most of that off the Laverman outfit, if only Higgins got to the finishing line in front.

Had we better start getting the last few bets on Father?

My bet last week was an even monkey with that Laverman bastard.

I had the same bet.

Do you know Tony, I think we're starting to put doubts in that feller's mind about the sanity of the whole business? When he laid my monkey Waterson told him to rub the price. Now has the man the courage of his convictions or what now would you say? We'll give him a couple of minutes and we'll start getting the rest of the cash on before Delgatty comes

Through the glass the bookmakers had begun erecting their stands. One had already begun chalking up advance prices on the final but the back of his board was to the men inside the bar.

There's Laverman.

Punch pointed without inhibition through the window.

Outside Laverman hovered around his pitch fussing as one of his entourage struggled to erect his betting stand. Every artist has an easel.

Come on Arthur. The first race'll be over before you get this bloody thing up.

The stand finally erected, Laverman started licking his chalk and shouting odds. Only the opening and closing of his mouth could be perceived by the men in the bar, like he was a goldfish only on the outside of the bowl.

Waterson knew Hurricane couldn't win but didn't want Laverman to put up a stupid price and raise the suspicions of the punters. He opted to play the market cautiously. He whispered to Laverman and, although the latter's money was not at stake, his adrenalin was surging. Like he said, the game was in his blood.

Here I'll take 11/8. I'll take 110/80 Hurricane. I'll take 11/8 the five dog.

Six or seven other bookmakers were betting early on the final and they pretty much all offered a more conservative 15/8 on. There was after all only one credible opponent to Higgins and that was the bitch Nemesis, priced at 9/4. She had encountered trouble at the first bend but finished strongly to win the other semi-final and her time put her only a couple of lengths behind Higgins. The other four dogs were 10/1 or bigger.

Father Ryan, Tony and Punch divided Delgatty's money in the gents and went out on to the steps in front of the bookmakers. They were witnesses to a sudden burst of activity in the betting line. The chalk marks disappeared one by one as the panic spread. One man steadfastly moved up the line taking any price he could about Nemesis.

One eighty to eighty the six. One eighty to eighty the bottom. Two hundred to one Nemesis. Five hundred to four the six. Even two hundred Nemesis.

Tic tacs flagged vehemently and hopelessly to their bookmaker colleagues.

Nothing the six dog. Nothing Nemesis. Nothing at all the bottom.

That's Judge ain't it?

Punch looked at Tony for confirmation and Father Ryan looked at them both.

What the fuck is he doing?

The Father approached the betting line. He knew what was going to happen next.

Waterson spoke into his boss's ear and Laverman addressed the ring.

Evens Hurricane! Even money Hurricane. Come on then five to four this good thing.

Nemesis crashed to odds-on favouritism.

Someone pushed in front of Father Ryan at Laverman's stand.

Eight hundred pounds on Higgins please.

A bet of this size at a permit track was practically unheard of. Waterson looked at Laverman.

Yeah, take it. One thousand to eight hundred the five dog.

Conrad wiped his ticket before placing it in his breast pocket. A single large daisy shone from his lapel.

Eight hundred pounds on Hurricane please.

Yoko was never far behind. She too sported a shasta daisy, with its yellow centre and large white petals, in her jacket lapel.

The priest stood his ground and did not proffer a bet. There was plenty of time to get the money on yet. They'd be betting on the final in between the next four races. Tony and Punch meantime settled for getting their bets on in smaller quantities down the line.

Fifty to forty. Fifty five to forty.

The priest spoke quietly into Tony's ear.

We should've known that would happen. The six dog would be a good thing in Hurricane's absence and he has every reason to believe he will be absent doesn't he though? Laverman and his lackey have had their brains on the striped jacket and Judge is putting the fucking money on for them. Would you believe it?

Betting on the big event was temporarily suspended as prepararations for the first race of the night got underway. The bell announced the runners were at the traps and queues filed out of both exits at the sides of the stand.

41.

Dogs to the paddock please for The Final of The Brownhills Derby.

Delgatty, waiting in the car park for the announcement, only caught the word *Final*.

Come on lad. We're on.

He opened the back of the car, holding the dog's head down as he allowed the hatch to rise gradually. His guts were aching as he released the animal. The dog bounded from the car on a tight lead and Delgatty held him in one stride. He locked the car and picked his way through the parked vehicles across the cinders watching for glass.

Father Ryan, Punch and Tony were waiting for him at the gate.

Just a minute Delgatty.

The Father pulled the other two men gently aside. They stood by the corrugated fence of the track.

Let's just take a minute in prayer you boys.

Tony looked to the heavens not so much in prayer as exasperation.

In the name of the Father and of the Son and of the Holy Ghost. Amen

Amen.

Amen.

Father we pray for our souls. We pray for forgiveness for the sins we have wittingly or...

Tony was anxious to get back into the track.

Just pray for the bloody dog Father,

I am going to pray for the dog Tony but we want to be able to pray with a clean soul……we have wittingly or unwittingly committed. We pray for the soul of Cadman.

Tony sighed. Delgatty smiled.

And now Father we ask for your blessing on our Higgins here in Trap 6.

Trap 5.

Tony couldn't help himself.

I mean Trap 5 Lord.

Father Ryan narrowed his eyes in Tony's direction.

Amen.

Amen.

Amen. Ok that's enough. Let's go.

Tony was first through the owners' gate.

Inside the betting ring Waterson didn't know what the fuck was going on. After all there should've been a withdrawl announced by now. The dog was certain not to run but why had he just been backed to the tune of an even two grand down the boards? It was the first time to his knowledge that a dead dog, an actual dead dog, had been so heavily supported in the market. Tonight's bets would have to be refunded over Hurricane's non-participation of course, but all the wagers over the past two weeks would stand and leave Waterson a healthy five grand or so profit.

Laverman had decided he would make his own money laying Nemesis and the other four dogs in the final.

Then Waterson caught sight of Delgatty with a dog. A black dog. A living black dog which clearly was not dead. He wanted to puke but was restrained by a touch of reason amidst the panic. He took his glasses off and wiped the sweat from his knitted eyebrows.

They're not getting away with no bastard ringer.

Within a minute Waterson was articulating something which, from Delgatty's viewpoint, was an hysterical mime into the racing manager's ear. But the recipient of the tirade only shook his head in reply; shook it in a way that was meant to reassure Waterson. But it wasn't the assurance he was looking for.

Rumours flirted in the air with flat caps talking to the backs of necks; the dog game with its gossips.

Hurricane has taken a walk in the market, drifting like a barge. All the money's for that Nemesis.

I've heard say that black dog is good enough to run in the Derby at White City.

Delgatty walked into the paddock and removed the dog's coat to weigh in.

Thirty five kilos.

Delgatty checked the kennel thoroughly to make sure it was clear and clean. There was no need to chain Hurricane in the racing kennel. He climbed on to the bed good as gold and Punch took up his position outside.

Laverman, some said, had been philanthropic with regards to Brownhills and he had built them a decent stand with a small restaurant and a couple of bars. Most believed it was a tax dodge, writing money off against the roulette winnings in his nightclub.

Delgatty passed Laverman and Waterson on his way to find Esther Marie.

Evening Mr. Laverman. Mr. Waterson.

Laverman ignored him. Waterson's hackles rose. He was seething and made no reply. He took himself off to the first bend and stood alone until the race was over.

Well Arthur, I might as well try and make a few quid on the race. Here you are then! Evens Nemesis. Evens the six dog in the final.

As he entered the bar Delgatty saw that the restaurant seats in the glass-fronted stand were filled. The view over the track was superb. The straights were cut like bowling greens and the white sanded bends, raked over after the previous race, lay unblemished like freshly ironed sheets. Outside the rutted car park, dotted with the white uniforms of stewards, was almost full.

He excused his way through the people standing crowded behind the diners and reached Esther Marie and Harriet at the bar. They had company in the form of Judge.

Are you OK Marie?

Yes I'm fine. Judge has been chatting to Harriet and me, distracting me ... you know.

Esther Marie was making good progress in the market place as it were.

Judge being sociable? That's a first.

Everything all right Delgatty?

Yes, why shouldn't it be?

Delgatty took his drink from Esther Marie and gripped a newly-lit cigar between his lips.

You don't usually smoke Castellas.

No Marie they only had these or Manikins and they're horrible. Castella is the cigar of the people. Sunday dinner times and sporting occasions. That right Judge?

Judge reverted to type and nodded disinterestedly.

42.

Father Ryan knew how to tell a good tale. Everyone in his Parish in County Cork had heard the story of the betting coup at Brownhills in April 1974 and Delgatty was revered even though hardly anybody had ever met him.

A certain mythology surrounded Delgatty. He was an avenging angel in the minds of the priest's flock. It was like a fifth gospel. Matthew, Mark, Luke, John and according to Ryan.

This bookmaker was shovelling money on the bitch Nemesis till about eight o'clock when Delgatty sure enough showed up with Higgins himself now. When Waterson saw the two of them, large as life, he looked like he was going to explode, yer know.

Anyways after much wailing and gnashing of teeth in the bookmaker's party, preparations for the race get underway. Delgatty coats up the dog in the orange jacket and takes Higgins to the traps himself. He slides him in gentle as you like in the box next to the bitch Nemesis. There's a bit of irony in that name I can tell you.

The men in the pub were aware of the irony.

Oh go on Father with the story.

The traps fly open and Nemesis in Trap 6 leads up and cuts across right in front of Higgins. He's nowhere to go so he switches to the outside. The one dog makes a burst up the rail and baulks the two. The three dog at 50/1 misses the trouble and finds himself disputing the fucking lead for God's sake. Higgins is in third round the first two bends and still keeping wide.

By the third bend Nemesis has a length on the field. The legs have fallen off the three dog and it's dropping away fast and the four looks like a threat now. This Nemesis is a strong finisher remember. She came from behind in all her heats and she's in front now.

All the time our Hurricane Higgins is holding the outside and running his guts out. He has a toe injury remember now.

Yes Father.

Nemesis looks like hanging on in the straight. The crowd are screaming and leaning across the rails and in the last couple of strides Higgins rallies and switches inside the bitch, the clever bastard, and they flash past the winning line together.

Nobody knows what's won. Waterson goes running back to Laverman and wants to try and limit the damage by laying Nemesis in the photo. But Skinner had been dead on the line - he knows exactly where to stand for the photo yer know - and he too comes running back to the ring and confides his knowledge to his usual bookmaker patrons. Nemesis is called by a couple of other books at 2/1 and Laverman shuts his bag and walks away.

I'm finished on this race Waterson. You'll have to take what comes, he says. I'm standing right in front of him yer know.

The thug takes of his sunglasses and his glass eye glows in the artificial light. He wipes his forehead with his hand. He's sweating like the fat pig that he is. And after four or five minutes when we're all thinking Skinner must've been wrong and it must at best be a dead heat, the announcement comes.

First Trap 5, Hurricane. Second Trap 6, Nemesis. Time 29.19. A new track record.

And by a short head, less than a short head I tell you, he's nailed the fucker on the line!

Father Ryan had a more sanitised version of the story for the Sunday School.

43.

Waterson took a wad from his inside jacket pocket and threw it petulantly into Laverman's bag. It was a wad, as they say in racing, big enough to choke a donkey. He nodded to another one of Laverman's men and the two of them directly left the track.

The party, gradually and excitedly, collected their winnings down the line of bookmakers but chiefly from Laverman. Laverman joked as he paid out; joked with relief. Although he had lost a few hundred quid on Nemesis, he had greatly reduced his liability on the bitch and he wasn't paying out his own money on Hurricane.

Delgatty diplomatically absented himself from the trophy presentation, as did Laverman. The thought of Laverman and Delgatty shaking hands appalled them both.

The smiling voice of the announcer echoed across the track.

The Brownhills Derby Cup will now be presented in the paddock by Mrs Claudia Laverman, representing her generous husband Mr Cyril Laverman, to the Misses Harriet and Esther Delgatty representing the owner-trainer, who also happens to be their brother, Mr. J. Delgatty.

There was a polite burst of applause and not a few whoops of delight from Delgatty's team. After the photographs of his sisters and the dog were taken, Delgatty hopped over the paddock rail, collected Higgins from the winner's podium, washed his feet in the paddock facility and, uncerimoniously, he too left the track.

44.

Delgatty got a brandy at the bar of *The Mulberry Tree* and took it into the beer garden, where he could keep an eye on Higgins in the car on the edge of the smaller of the two car parks. It was nearly ten o'clock, close to last orders, and everyone else was inside the pub shunning the nip in the April air. He lit a cigar and blew the smoke to the night. Maybe Waterson would come looking for him.

A figure entered the garden.

Jay? Is that you?

Yes it's me Marie.

Thank God. I was worried. You just disappeared from the track.

Delgatty walked over to his younger sister and embraced her. They stood in silence for some moments until they were joined by Harriet carrying two glasses of wine from the pub.

Well done Jay. You pulled it off brilliantly!

Harriet kissed him.

At *The Mulberry Tree* there are two car parks. The main one is to the front of the pub and is additionally obscured from the large, rear garden by trees and shrubs where two cars now held five silent occupants. Tony spoke.

How do they know where to come?

Judge pushed himself up on the steering wheel of his Mini.

Delgatty told Waterson himself that he comes here after racing. Anyway one of them has been following him for a fortnight. They know where to come all right. Waterson left the track straight after the result was called with another couple of thugs.

Judge wound his window down and Yoko did the same from the rear passenger seat in Conrad's car which, although not quite a hearse, was long and black.

Tony opened the hinged, rear window of the Mini so he could hear what was being said.

Are you sure Delgatty will be in the garden Judge?

Yes sure. He always goes there after racing at Brownhills. Don't you listen?.

Punch opened his passenger door and unfolded his great frame on to the tarmac.

I hope they ain't gonna be all night Judge. I wanna coke.

Tony laughed.

You're about to get your fucking head kicked in and you want a coke?

Fucking head kicked in and you want a coke?

Yoko smiled as she said it and the others roared. It was communal barking to relieve the tension.

Conrad and Yoko climbed out of their funereal limousine, each peering at themselves in the gloomy wing mirrors on either side of the vehicle. The two cars looked like a solemn father and son with their extinguished headlights and unsmiling radiator grilles.

A black cab turned into the car park. It was Azad. He alighted from his vehicle and his strange Persian garb shone alternately white and black in the flashing neon light of the pub.

Tony greeted his new friend enthusiastically.

I'm so glad you came tonight Azad. How did you find us here though?

Oh we taxi drivers have a bloody knack, you know.

He's got a bloody knack all right.

Father Ryan climbed out of the back of the cab.

Their laughter was interrupted by the slow arrival of a white Transit van. The side door slid open and Waterson and three other heavies emerged looking simultaneously purposeful and uncertain. The passenger door opened and another hood introduced himself to the night. He held a shot gun. The driver slammed his door and joined them.

Judge approached the driver. He remembered the black and white films of his youth.

You got a light mate?

What you doing here Judge? I wouldn't hang about if I was you. It's going to get messy.

Oh I think I will hang about though. Punch'll look after me won't you Punch?

The boxer walked forward from the shadows.

Yeah.

Waterson, at the head of the gang, lowered his head, seemingly confused by the numbers confronting him and fixed the focus of his single eye on the biggest target, Punch. He rushed at the boxer. Tony and Mary threw their slight bodies in his path to limit the pace and damage of his charge. Now he was alongside Punch who floored him with one swipe and drew blood.

Punch lifted the thug with one hand. He put his other arm on Waterson's shoulder and the one-eyed man felt the weight of this hostile gesture and, maybe for once in his life, he was afraid.

Waterson raised himself to his feet. He stood, staring unseeingly about him, wounded, breathless. The saliva hung from his jowells. Enraged he shook his bloody head and the red sweat flew off him.

Punch challenged him.

Was it you in the van that killed Terry Cadman?

The thug charged again, blindly this time, into the whole assembly, knocking Tony off his feet.

Fucking hell!

And then the fighting began with an almost balletic choreography. Punch thumped another of Waterson's cronies.

Ryan and Azad looked at each other.

Good thoughts, good words, good deeds eh Azad?

As he spoke the Father punched one of the hoods in the belly whilst Azad swung around his neck and shouted.

There's a time and a place Father. We can't stand by.

Tony, incensed at being dashed to the ground, gathered himself and launched his small frame into the reluctant embrace of the armed man. The shotgun went off scattering the doves into the black sky from the high trees.

Conrad and Yoko waved their arms without making much contact with anyone apart from, on one occasion, each other. Judge swung out in all directions with his skinny arms.

One by one the mob were desperate to return to their vehicle and get out of there. Before they did, Punch got hold of the groggy Waterson by his hair, and held him for Judge to pass sentence.

This is the end of it you understand. This is the fucking end or you're going down. We know about Cadman. We know about the dog. We stand together with Delgatty. We are one. Make sure you understand. Come near us again and Punch will put your other fucking eye out.

Waterson was escorted, by his debilitated entourage, from the scene of his ignominy; half stooping, half running his way back to the van. The van sped into the Staffordshire night.

The small party of men and women, high on the adrenaline of victory, made their way into the garden. The umistakable bulk of Punch led the way. Conrad followed with Yoko, both of them flicking their hair back into something like its previous, immaculate shape. Father Ryan and Azad walked together, their arms around each others' shoulders. Tony and Mary skipped along at the rear with laughter in their light steps. Delgatty stood to greet them.

Delgatty hadn't known about the fight and thought the shouting had been down to departing revellers and that the shotgun was a rogue pigeon scarer.

A job well done tonight boys and girls.

You can say that again.

Tony dabbed at his bloody nose with his sleeve. Mary handed him her silk hanky.

Where's Penny, Tony?

The whole bunch responded.

Penny says she'll come later!

Because of this choral response, Azad thought this must be some sort of prayer and reacted automatically.

Amen.

Father Ryan gave him a friendly thump on the back.

And Amen from me too.

As the laughter died away, Delgatty approached Judge.

What about Mr. Cadman, Judge?

I didn't even know Cadman, Delgatty. Sure I'd seen him on the slope at Wolves but I'd never spoken to him. I am very sorry for what happened to him. Laverman asked me if Cadman was involved in that gamble and I said I couldn't imagine it. I feel ashamed now but I said I thought he was just a guesser, a con man. Look I wouldn't have come here tonight if I wasn't on your side Delgatty, Marie, Harriet.

It's a good job I'm here to keep an eye on you Delgatty if you want the truth. Waterson swallowed the whole fucking thing. He had worked out you'd go to Kidderminster though and most likely when. He wanted to go but I told him I knew the place and I'd go. He trusted me.

Esther Marie looked angry. She was very angry.

And what about Rex? Did you know about Rex, Judge? Did Laverman or Waterson or whoever they are, trust you about that too?

Marie.

He searched for the words but there weren't any that could make up for her loss. He tried.

Laver.... Laverman is not a killer. He's on the dodgy side but he's essentially a business man. It's all figures to him. It's all about odds.

It was the greatest regret to me that Rex was killed and you must believe I knew nothing at all about it or I would certainly have warned you. I would have done more. If I'd known I would have tried to prevent it. I know for a fact Laverman knew nothing about it. He probably still doesn't. All he knew was that Waterson kept throwing money in the bag to lay Higgins.

You mean Waterson killed Rex. He didn't even tell Laverman about it? Laverman knew nothing about Rex?

He knew nothing Marie. That's why he chalked up a normal book on the final. He was expecting Higgins to turn up. He couldn't believe it when Waterson kept telling him to lay Higgins. Waterson believed Higgins was dead but he couldn't say anything without admitting his part in it.

I believe you Judge. You never know another's motives.

Tony warmed to his theme.

A man's agenda is his own.

Delgatty smiled at Tony in a way that Tony knew to shut up and he put his hand on his sister's shoulder.

She persisted.

Was all that barney with Judge in the car park at the track just a show, Jay?

Maybe it was Marie but it wasn't planned. It sort of made sense at the time. I just got carried away and thought Judge had joined the opposition. I should have realised that he was there just to put the money on for them. I don't know. It was as if the plan developed a mind of its own. Like it was out of our hands. It worked better than I could ever have planned it. Things moved beyond our own instigation, mine and Judge's.

They each reflected on the ordeal of the last few weeks in a brief, heavy silence. Esther Marie found herself beginning to thaw a little in her response to Judge.

Father Ryan cut into the silence.

Judge was betting for them again tonight.

Father Ryan spoke as if this were the final revelatory nail in Judge's coffin. Tony nodded in agreement.

Yeah you did though Judge.

Punch was embarrassed to make such a claim after the stalwart efforts of the sinewy man in the combat.

Yeah you did Judge.

Course I was fucking betting for them Father, Tony, Punch. The more the bastards lost the better wasn't it? Don't let's lose sight of what we've done here, what Delgatty has done, what Hurricane has done. Delgatty, you are a genius.

Judge kissed him on the cheek.

Delgatty had almost the final word.

Things are still raw, I know. Sacrifices have been made. Very big sacrifices have been made. When a dog is killed the world is changed.

Azad nodded his agreement.

When you kill a man you change the universe.

Everyone maintained a silence.

But we can celebrate quietly tonight and one day soon we will have a spectacular celebration.

Yeah with all the fuckin' money we won.

Punch broke the mood perfectly. They all laughed. They laughed sincerely. Nobody barked. They did celebrate in a quiet way. They had to as the bar was now closed. The bell had rung out twice across the April night air, first for last orders and then for home time.

The Delgattys passed their glasses of wine and brandy around like chalices. Each of their friends, even the teetotalers, took a sacramental sip and toasted Cadman and Dexter. They toasted Rex and Higgins. They toasted each other. And everything in the garden, for now, was lovely.

The black, April buds on the mulberry flashed white in the neon.